THE MUSIC OF SOLITUDE

THE MUSIC OF SOLITUDE

KRISHNA SOBTI

Translated from the Hindi by
Vasudha Dalmia

HARPERPERENNIAL

First published in English in India in 2013 by Harper Perennial
An imprint of HarperCollins *Publishers*

HarperCollins Publishers India, Cyber City, Building 10-A, Gurugram,
Haryana-122002, India
www.harpercollins.co.in

2 4 6 8 10 9 7 5 3 1

This edition published in India in 2019 by Harper Perennial

First published in Hindi in 2000 as *Samay Sargam* by Rajkamal Prakashan

P-ISBN: 978-93-5302-492-5
E-ISBN: 978-93-5302-661-5

Typeset in Joanna MT 11/14
Jojy Philip New Delhi 110 015

Printed and bound at
MicroPrints India, New Delhi

MIX
Paper
FSC FSC™ C218906

This product is made of FSC®-certified and other controlled material.

HarperCollins Publishers, Macken House, 39/40 Mayor Street
Upper, Dublin 1, D01 C9W8, Ireland

one

The window curtain flapped wildly in the wind.

Was a dust storm on the way?

A dust storm in winter?

No.

She tucked the curtain into the window grill and looked out. The wan afternoon light flickered in the strong wind. In the distance, the dome of Humayun's tomb basked in its arc of sunlight. The warmth of the winter sun lightly brushed her clothes. The endless drama of existence, and on such a vast stage.

This earth, the sky, the sun, the winds, and us.

What remained to be enacted on this stage?

Aranya's breathing quickened. The dream she had last night replayed itself in her mind. What a scene!

Somewhere in the sky a large door had become visible. A massive door set in a wooden frame, with Aranya's nameplate fixed on it.

A small door within the door opened, and a familiar face peeped out.

Who?

Why, it's me! It's me peeping out from behind that small door.

No, no, that can't be. I'm standing outside!

Look carefully, Aranya. Isn't that wrinkled face yours?

It is indeed. So what? We grow older by the moment, don't we?

Yes. But you must know that these are not lines of torment. They've grown and ripened with time. The time we ourselves lived through.

Such smugness. Then why this q and a! Are you examining the door? You created it, by the sheer act of living.

Aranya locked her hands together.

She unlocked them after a while and touched her hair, to connect with herself again.

Are you anxious about something?

No, I'm taking the air in. Pulling in the oxygen, all the way to my soul, glad that I'm alive; my companions, they all left, a long time ago.

Those faces … No, forget them. Say goodbye to them and to the memories of those who are living but are no longer what they once were, those who died and were reborn—I'm content to be alive.

Aranya looked around the room. The fruits lying on the table tugged at her with their colours and fragrance; she was mesmerized by them. She picked up a knife and a plate, and began to peel them in a leisurely manner.

The bowl began to fill with sliced fruit. She squeezed some lemon and sprinkled salt and a little black pepper. Then she tasted a slice and added a spoonful of sugar.

Forget the dream. Take joy in the freshness of these fruits. Everything is the same as yesterday. Resting on its axis. What if it moves? But there's time … The last halt—that business can overtake one anytime. It will. It has to happen. It happens to everyone.

Are you brooding over that? The string you're looking for is wound around a pulley fixed to that door high above; why look for it here? Are you frightened?

Yes and no, both.

Try and relax as long as you can. Take pleasure in the seasons. This breeze doesn't exist elsewhere. Not even on the moon.

With a light heart, she picked up the receiver and called Ishan. The phone rang for a long time. She dialled the number again after an hour. It rang and was picked up.

Hello!

Hello, I was about to hang up. I thought you were resting.

It was clean-the-toilet day today. Just finished. Would you like to go for a walk to the park this evening?

Yes, I'd like to come. What time?

Four-thirty sharp. We'll meet at the gate.

Aranya felt flustered. She must rest before going for the walk. I'm feeling quite tired. Forgot to take my vitamins this morning.

She thought as she rested: who knows how we interpret the movement of the hands of a clock.

Ishan lives in terror of the clock, his gaze always fixed on it, while I steal my eyes away from it.

But why compare; each gait has its own pace.

Aranya went downstairs at precisely twenty-five past four.

She looked at her wrist. Dot on time! It's not so easy to escape its claws. Particularly for this senior person whose keys go missing sometimes, or her purse, or her cardigan. Or she's caught in the quandary of whether to wear light clothes or heavy; heavy will make walking more difficult, light may mean feeling cold. Ancient body!

Walking on the street, she looked at herself again. Quick and alert. Clothes neither too warm nor too cool. It's a pleasure to carry one's own weight this way.

The long row of keekar trees lining the street sway in the shimmering sunlight. Fields of ripening mustard below the concrete embankment. Small and middling plants engrossed in the business of drawing in sunlight and air. The traffic on the street whizzing past, oblivious of all this.

Ishan parked the car. They walked to the park gate. The tall eucalyptus trees looked dejected, even at that lofty altitude. Perhaps because they were outside the park. On the pavement to their right were mounds of gravel and rubble. There was barbed wire along the hedge surrounding the park. Through this, a narrow lane entered the park.

There's a slope here, be careful. Will you be able to leap over it?

Oh yes.

Two pairs of shoes, put on the alert, entered the park cautiously. A long row of red sandstone, surrounded by the green of ashoka trees. Flowerbeds accompanying them, like string instruments. Tiny phlox, red, pink, purple, white. Ahead of them, a cluster of vines. Of bougainvillea, bright red and pink, and noble Brazilian palms. The ones behind, a lesser breed, stand apart. There are differences even in a park. Mandal's caste politics is in play here as well!

The grass is like a green spread; its dharma, the protection of its greenness. But it's not averse to a sprinkling of colours. The circular flowerbeds are a riot of colours; without a trace of fragrance, but swaggering nonetheless. Dwarf morpankhi shrubs, interlinked and attached to their own species, and woven together with vivacious leaves. There should have been a marble platform in front of them—they would aquire a different charm and glory then.

Senior citizens sit and chat in a grove on elevated ground. Their public debates take place outside the bounds of their homes and families. The cumulative solitude of years gone by.

Ishan and Aranya pause at the bend in the path. From this point on, they'll go different ways.

We'll come back and meet here exactly at six.

Aranya strode off to the left. The branches of the weeping willow droop. Glistening amongst them is the red bottlebrush, and beyond, long rows of teak trees.

The park looks like a series of paintings in the evening light. The breeze revolves slowly like a windmill. The yellow crowns of trees glitter on the waves of the wind.

The trees beyond the mosque stay calm, laden with their own capricious branches. Who knows what the flocks of birds are saying to each other? No one needs to pay a price for this din. Can it compete with the blare of cars whose wheels move only if petrol is used and paid for? These channels vibrate without taxes.

Could this be the way in which the mute trees express their resistance?

Against whom would that be? Against the creepers that cling to them?

No, these trees oppose us two-legged ones. Perhaps they are fed up with our whimsies.

And what about the birds? There's no one to curb the flock of feathered ones. They chirp and twitter endlessly, tormenting the wise old trees. Producing a mighty din, they sing whole arias, flaunting taans. The aging trees remain silent; they say nothing. Entirely spiritual, that's what they are. No, no, they are secretive—always spying on the sly.

Suddently, a neelkanth took flight.

Waah, what wings, what a flight!

Tiny blades of grass began to sway in the wind.

Aranya broke into a hasty trot, almost running, and hit her foot against an upturned stone; a tile had broken loose.

Take care! You'll fall. You're not all that young. There can be an accident, any time.

She suddenly remembered the insurance papers.

You have kept them carefully, no?

She'll have to look for them the moment she gets back.

Some of the walkers looked at her with surprise as she broke into a trot. Such pace at this age! Involuntarily, she slowed down.

She looked at her watch and spotting an empty bench in the distance, she reserved it with her eyes. She would rest when she got there. The lawn was being watered. She took off her shoes and socks and, cutting sideways across the lawn, reached her destination.

The creepers, branches and twigs began to darken. What had looked like watercolours in the thin sunlight a while ago now looked like dark oil paint. The Almighty has boundless freedom. He has done countless experiments with his universe. Each thing has its own nature, quality and form.

A tree is different from a creeper, flower from leaf, deer from cheetah, cheetah from rabbit, butterfly from peacock, peacock from crow, crow from sparrow, man from lion, lion from child, child from mother, mother from father.

Strange and wonderful, this world of the Almighty—his and ours.

Ishan is coming towards her.

Aranya began to pull on her socks.

Have your shoes been hurting you?

No. The grass was wet and I needed to protect my shoes. So I carried them in my hands.

Ishan laughed.

Is there any sense in protecting your shoes and catching a cold? You may end up having to take antibiotics.

Aranya laughed.

Before that, I'll have drunk a *kaadha* of black pepper, tulsi and liquorice.

That's a good habit. It's not good to pop too much medication.

The moral of the story is that it's not good for a senior citizen like me to walk on wet grass.

Yes, Aranya, senior citizens can end up paying a heavy price for such carelessness.

You're right. In the future then, only Action shoes for me.

Add another phrase to that, otherwise you'll end up sounding like a shoe brand commercial.

No, an evening like this can't end with a commercial.

Let's have a conversation about spirituality then.

Aranya, does this word exist in your dictionary?

Don't think so. My lot is known for fighting for its rights, and yours for trying to achieve peace and clarity for all living beings by means of knowledge and wisdom.

Yes, but you seem all set to engage in a verbal duel. Are you getting ready for a battle?

Do I look very aggressive? Ah, yes, the activity of the subconscious mind shows in the tapping of feet.

Discipline—

Yes, I too have that. You own the arsenal of science and I, weapons.

You're the one who is making the distinction.

The whole country is caught up in the commotion of caste history. I'm a Brahman, I'm non-Brahman. I'm Kshatriya, I'm a Rajput, I'm Jat-Gujar, I'm from a backward caste, I'm Dalit, I'm Scheduled Caste.

Hang on, wherever did Indianness go?

It went to the scales of the judiciary.

Why don't we change the subject?

Let's talk about happiness-beyond-belief.

You go first.

The list of what makes me happy is very short. In one line: a cluster of words and the expression of meaning. Nothing more. Now, your turn.

The pleasure of reading a good book.

Let's hear a bit more about that.

The pleasure of sighting the consciousness glistening behind words—crystalline consciousness, whose transparent gleam never fades.

Are you saying this in your individual context?

Yes, that is the most irreplaceable dimension of human life. A complete creation. To be conscious of oneself is re-creation. Am I right?

Yes, I know what you mean.

We are reborn each time we refashion ourselves, renew ourselves.

Aranya silently asked herself: How many times might you have been born? Many times! Truly, this one life had in itself many launch pads for many births.

To rescue them from the long silence that followed, Ishan said,You say something. It's your turn now.

A rebirth is underway these days as well. In the act of shredding paper. It foretells age. Have you been through this experience too?

Yes. Sometimes old letters, sometimes old accounts, calendars, diaries. And if I'm to speak of myself, along with papers, memories as well. Perhaps that's what people call nirvana.

Why insist on so much plain speaking?

Because I live in colloquial prose.

They strolled in the rose garden.

The language of poetry seems to grow in this little garden.

I have come here before.

Did you see the dusky rose-daughter in the red-orange flower patch?

That's a beautiful name, rose-daughter. There isn't any feminist influence working on this identification, is there?

That may well be. Sons form the majority in this park. We worry about the minorities. That's why it's so important to note the existence of daughters.

Ishan laughed.

This shouldn't get us tangled in an argument.

No, that won't happen. Why would we trade our expansive vision for insularity? Regardless of quarrels, we seniors will ultimately attain peace.

They laughed.

But even there, the goddess of desires will block the passage of rights.

I see what you're getting at. We will all face her infinite power.

Ishan laughed again. You could need a lawyer even there.

There must be some arrangement. The prosecution will work, if we pay the fees. But the verdict may take time.

It could take eons.

Several centuries may go by while you wait.

Aranya broke into a peal of laughter.

It feels good to hear we'll live that long. Let me tell you, I'm ready to wait patiently; I'm not willing to let go of my rights.

Their voices began to fade as the sounds of the evening took over.

The greenish light in the park turned blue. The last evening light just before it gets dark.

What's your favourite colour?

Black.

No, no, that's not the colour of joy.

Why not? That's the colour I liked in the pink of my youth. Now I wear grey and white. These two colour my interior.

They walked in silence. Suddenly Aranya laughed.

Please don't think I've reached my grey years. Although, human beings harbour many desires even beyond the grey.

A flower patch snaked its way right up to the gate. Together they leapt over it.

Time is wordless, but much throbs within. And age? It's like a goat, grazing, slowly, slowly. Let it graze. Don't look in its direction.

Aranya asked herself softly: You haven't become more shortsighted, have you? You must get eye-drops from the chemist. When is your next appointment with the eye-doctor?

She heard Ishan say: Seems like I'll need to change my distance-glasses.

The golden face of the sun shines in the deep blue of the sky. The east end of the park departs to meet the sky as the face of the west lights the eyes. As if east and west are saying to one another: Today will surely resemble yesterday. But tomorrow won't be like today.

In the west, the sun, a red ball of fire, slides towards the Earth that is like a stage.

Behind it, there is a vast curtain of darkness. A redness flickers for a split-second in our lashes and disappears into the Earth.

The trees are quieter than before, dumbfounded by their own immeasurable height. Entranced by their own imperishability perhaps. And the two of us, aging perishables.

The cobbled footpath has begun to look new. No old memories, no reproaches, no rivalry, no aggression, no civilities. Just walking together, the two of us. It's good to walk. That's what the doctor says as well.

Aranya spoke sternly to herself. You keep coming back to that. Doctor.

Look at the tree trunks, firmly anchored in their roots.

Watch where you are going. Take firmer steps. This is a journey towards unexpected connections. Its pace is determined by one's own being and living. By the sound of one's own footsteps, not the shifting of the planets.

The cool breeze blows only as long as we live. No enmeshment. No east wind, north wind, or south. Who knows when the winds flew off in their own directions? What remains will also fly off. Whatever is right for the season; there is a meaning to everything. The right thing has to be understood in the right way at the right time. Look ahead of yourself. The sun has sunk and amidst the trees, there's the moon, hanging in its cage of desire. Being able to see that is an event, isn't it.

Aranya reached her floor. She opened the door to her flat, switched on the light and stood in the balcony. The wide banks of the Yamuna fringed with lights. The windows of flats near and far. Windows, it's not windows that change. It's the curtains, faces, and dates that change. She went inside and took off her shoes. She washed her feet, and as she wiped them with a towel, she saw a few blades of grass sticking to her soles.

She gazed at them for a while. How tiny. She plucked them off carefully. How slender to touch. That sprint on the wet grass was wonderful. The accomplishment for the evening.

She filled water in the kettle and switched it on.

Looked into the tea-tin and found it empty.

There would be teabags. There were some. That's how organized we loners are. If there's tea, there's no sugar; if there's sugar, there's no milk. Lack of structure and order.

No, let's not complain today. Teabags have appeared, and so have milk and sugar.

She placed the tea tray in front of herself, and then drank the tea, regarding herself as a guest. An actor, onlooker, audience, guest, host, all rolled into one.

The phone rang.

Hello.

This is Ishan.

Tell me.

Just look outside your door.

Aranya rose swiftly. Had a guest arrived? She turned the key and peeped outside. A paper bag was hanging from the doorknob. She took it down and shut the door. There were flowers in the bag, and tucked into them was a slip of paper: 'For not getting your shoes wet in the park.'

Aranya was happy. These lovely little pieces of happiness … The new shoes were saved from getting wet. At the same time, she managed to impress someone and received a bunch of narcissus.

She filled water in the vase, arranged the flowers, and played music. She sat there, listening for a while, and then danced to the tune, as if old times began tapping in her feet.

Nothing is forgotten. Practise remembering.

Will you be able to add another line to the script, at this juncture in your life?

Yes, of course—just this much that I am my own script.

Much later, she thought, I could have phoned and thanked him. No. Let this remain unsaid. I'm feeling special. I've just received the flowers of narcissus for a gift. These bloom on the mountains where silence swims in the air.

The sky was overcast since morning. It began to rain by the time the afternoon was over. Perhaps it had snowed in the mountains. Aranya kept admiring the duet of shower and wind from her balcony. The tar on the street down below looked dark and smooth from this height. The canopy of leaves on the trees below appeared like green pavilions, bowing towards the earth and opening towards the sky.

How ancient the sight and sound of the shower and how eternally new. Time is concealed in its melody. Time is, because we are. Time is outside but also ahead of us. That is what intimidates us. But why dither on this rainy day?

Grasp this moment; it is yours. The evening, this moment, this rain—jump up and gather them in your hands. If you slip now, they may slip away forever.

Aranya picked up her umbrella and raincoat and set out in the rain. New roads had been laid out in front of the flats. One can't look for the past on them. Who knows how many have been left behind? A big pool of water splashed under her feet. Watch out! Your shoes will get dirty. She sprang to the side.

New plants had been planted along the pavement on the right. Propped up with bricks, fresh saplings from the nursery.

Ahead, there was a tangled cluster of jhuggis, huddled under slanted roofs made of sacking and blue and yellow plastic, just wide enough to hide your heads, and held to the ground by ends tucked into stones. From the ones made by shutting off the openings of barrels, emerges, along with the wet smoke from a coal sigri, the sound of a child crying. The dry sobbing of a child rolling on a half wet mud floor. The rain must be dripping in. The mother must be looking for a way to stop the leaking.

Where will the child go after it grows out of the jhuggi? Will this Abhimanyu be able to escape his chakravyuha? Will he be able to emancipate himself from hustling narcotics or will he be crushed by the weight of generations? Will he be able to enter a clean brick house? Will he partake in the comforts of life? Will the imperial gaze of history manage to take note of him while there is still time? Will buying things at the Sunday flea market rescue him? Will he be able to fulfill his desire to buy new old-looking denims? Will the favours meted out by social welfare reach this puny citizen? Will the strength to sustain himself survive that long? He has sixteen to eighteen years to reach adulthood. It may be possible to become a politician in the next century. Who knows whether he'll behave like a hero or a villain?

It had begun to rain harder. The umbrella in Aranya's hands was beginning to fly off. She crossed the street to walk on the pavement on the opposite side. A heap of garbage suddenly appeared from nowhere. She shrank away but its stench smeared this part of the street. Strange is our relationship to garbage and clutter, and the indifference to its relentless aggression.

Aranya reprimanded herself: Don't look at the filthy mound of trash. Watch the water flow, see the lightening flash. Then she cautioned herself: Better go back.

As she entered the gate, she changed her mind about going back to her own flat. She could have a cup of tea with her friend and neighbour Ishan.

There was a spring in her steps. She shook the water off her umbrella, and crossing the passageway, pressed the lift button. It would have been better to phone him first, but that could be forgiven in this weather.

She placed her finger on the doorbell.

The door opened, but there was neither surprise nor joy on his face, only acceptance.

Perhaps it wasn't right to come, she thought to herself.

Ishan took the umbrella from her, put it in the balcony, and hung the raincoat in the bathroom.

Sorry, I think I've come at the wrong time. I thought of having tea with you as I was returning from my walk.

Why not! Come in.

I'll make the tea if you like.

No, no, you'll get the kind of tea you like. You've no restrictions regarding cinnamon and cardamom, have you?

No, none.

The sound of a kettle and spoons in the kitchen.

How much sugar?

Half-a-spoon.

Two mugs of tea were set down on the table. Biscuits and savouries on a plate.

Please help yourself.

Aranya lifted the mug. She took a sip and cast a glance around the room. A bit bare. Even though there are things here, it seems as if there aren't any. The face opposite hers is contained in itself and joined to itself.

You went for a walk in the rain? That was daring. It was a heavy shower.

A second later, he said: I wonder why I never thought of it. One could have gone for a walk.

He sat silently for a while, as if regretting his mistake. The empty cups brought him back to the present.

Would you like more tea?

Thanks, no.

Ishan rose and fetched a bundle of old exercise books and books from the next room.

I don't know why I thought of opening old boxes today. My son's things have been locked away for who knows how long. As I woke up this morning I felt an urge to open them today. See, these cuttings from magazines, stamp album, diary—

Death that defeats human beings, what colour must it be? That which smothers flying birds so that they disappear forever, forever out of our sight.

See here, a list of books. Which book read in which week, how many books in a month, and how many in a year. It's all been registered. The sayings he liked, the aphorisms, where he'd read them and from where he got them—all in great detail, in the style of a report. When the three of us set out to travel for the last time in the South, the moment we left Delhi, he started writing about it in this thick register.

Ishan was looking at his son, as if oblivious to Aranya's presence.

He had unusual eyes, large ears, and a fantastic memory.

Aranya picked up the green register and began to turn its pages, as if she couldn't hear what was being said nor read what she saw on the pages.

Had the guest's indifference been taken note of?

The empty mugs were removed from the table. Ishan went out into the balcony and peeped outside. Looks like it has stopped raining.

Aranya stood up to leave: I'm off.

Bahadur is not coming today. I am making a light dinner. Let's eat here. Everything's ready. I just need to put the pressure cooker on the gas stove.

Not today, another time, Ishan.

Why not today? Chance has brought us together today. I need just half an hour to walk. You can browse through a book or listen to music in the meanwhile. You'll find one or the other cassette that you like.

After Ishan left, Aranya sat there dejectedly for a while. The room felt deserted first, and then, as if it was suddenly stuffed full with a heap of things which had lain concealed before.

The decision to come here began to seem strange. She played the cassette lying on top of the pile and then switched it off in some confusion. She went and stood near the open boxes. In one of them were a colouring set, a pastel album, a geometry box, a camera ... of some unknown child who had ceased to be.

He, who is no more, peeps out of old things ... What relationship could he have with the stranger now looking at him? Chessmen, ludo, scout uniform, cap, whistle hanging out of a shirt pocket. Can it still blow? No, it's struck dumb. Only if there is breath within can the lips move.

Misfortune feels no pity. Not even in the face of love. And even though these memories have been preserved, they are dead. After the body is gone, if at all anything remains, it's memory. Nothing else. Step outside the dexterity of life and you're gone.

Another box—a jersey, a muffler, and a small button sewed on to the muffler. A school bag, high boots, a writing pad. As Aranya lifted the pad, a page fluttered out of it. A letter.

St Columba's School
Lunchtime

Hello Chote Mama,
I've been thinking of writing to you for some days. You know my friend Pradip, don't you? I've told you about him. He's very clever and he's good at studies. I'm about to write about his sacred thread ceremony. Mamma, Papa and I were invited to it. The family members and guests were sitting in a big room. The basin with the havan flames was in the middle. Pradip was dressed like a sadhu. His uncle, who was officiating as the pandit, was reading the mantras at a speed which would have put Kennedy to shame. His enunciation was truly impressive, the kind only pandits can bring forth. But yes, the smoke from the fire was a torture to our eyes. I rummaged in my pocket for the handkerchief I had forgotten at home. The ghee that Pandit-ji was putting into the fire was meagre. Perhaps the ghee was real, *asli ghee*, and Pandit-ji was being stingy. By then, instead of flames, clouds of smoke collected and enveloped the room. I was watching silently. Every now and then,

Papa would wipe his eyes with a handkerchief. Mamma was sitting in the verandah outside, so she was all right. Lunch was served afterwards. As I was eating, I thought I would never have the *yajnopavit* ceremony. I will not do this or allow Mamma's family to do this to me. And if Dadaji says something, I'll have an answer ready for him—if Papa didn't have his done, why do I have to? So, Chote Mama, you'll be saved from the smoke of my *yajnopavit*. You must write to me and let me know what you think of my decision.

I'll close this letter now. I'm going off to play. Please answer my letter, Chote Mama.

With love,
Yours,
Lavi.

The paper was beginning to crumble. The handwriting was neat, the mark of a good school. The letter must have been written on the school lawn during the lunch break.

Sliding the album of photos back into the suitcase, Aranya went to the bookshelf. She pulled out a book with a colorful cover. She heard a sound as she began to turn its pages, as if someone were murmuring into her ear.

Who?

It's me.

Who are you?

A friend of your Papa's. I live nearby. I had gone for a walk in the rain. I stopped on the way back.

And Papa?

He's gone for a walk.

Ha-ha-ha …

Did Aranya hear a child laugh?

I know it so well. Papa never misses a walk. I've walked with him. From Curzon Road Hostel to India Gate. I used to go with him every Sunday. One day, just as we were reaching the Boat Club, it started to rain in torrents. Ma was also with us. A big hailstone fell on us, and fat raindrops too. We stood under a tree, getting wet. We had gone under it for shelter, but its big leafy branches were beginning to break in the storm, and Ma and Papa were trying to protect their heads while I hid between them.

When the storm abated a bit, I began to tease Ma: Look Ma, a flying saucer is on its way here from over the stadium.

Ma and Papa looked in that direction as if a flying saucer could really be seen there.

You can see aliens sitting in them, can't you?

Ma said: God is ever active. He manifests himself in various forms.

Ma, we're talking about science.

Yes, yes, science and knowledge are controlled by God.

I looked at Papa and smiled. Sky, earth, nether worlds, they are all God's laboratories. Scientists have found a way to reach them. Papa, I'll set up my little laboratory in the skies. I'll interview the folks who come into outer space and send news of them to the papers here.

I am not sure why Ma and Papa became silent. I continued to talk, but they remained silent.

At dinner Ma asked: Son, whom do you feel closest to?

Myself.

What?

Yes, Ma, there is me, right? With me, with my name. With you, Papa, Dada, Dadi.

Why not your Nana?

He has his own grandsons.

Papa smiled but Ma got angry. Who are your friends ? Whom do you talk to?

Ma, can't I know things myself?

Yes, you know a lot of things, also things your Papa and I don't know.

I guessed what my mother was getting at.

I'm not competing with you. I'm your son after all. Don't you recognize me? This boy who goes to school and who comes home in the evenings, gets good marks in school and is sitting right here, in front of you? No, Papa?

Mama broke into a smile. Papa looked at me, unblinkingly. I saw that he wasn't angry with me. No praise when he was happy with me, no rebuke when he was annoyed. That's my Papa.

Before I went to sleep, Papa was more affectionate than on most days. He spoke to my mother when he thought I'd fallen asleep: Did you hear what your son was saying?

Whatever he was saying made me anxious. These are not the thoughts of a child. We should talk to Lavi's class teacher.

Ma gave me a closed envelope for Father Joseph next morning.

Son, don't forget to give this to Father Joseph. I've asked for an appointment with him.

Have I done something wrong, Ma?

No, you don't have to comment on everything grown-ups do.

Papa dropped me off to school. As he was leaving, I said: Ma is upset about nothing. What if I left this envelope with you?

Papa looked at me, mischievously. Your mother has just asked to see your class teacher, son. How can you object to that?

I understood. Papa was also party to this; it wasn't Ma alone. Let them both do what they want.

Bye-bye, Papa.

Aranya sat back in her chair, as if exhausted.

Bye, little one. You and I hadn't met before today. You must have been good at studies, your exercise books show that. And what you were just talking about—

What makes you say that? It was you talking. I was just listening.

Dinner was laid on the table. Soup, steamed vegetables, yoghurt, fruits, a jar each of honey and lemon juice.

Aranya began to read the jar with her eyes. Honey-lemon, lemon-honey. In this weather, on this wet evening.

I can add brandy to it, if you like.

Thanks, I'd like that.

Did anyone knock while I was away? Srinivas was supposed to come.

No.

Aranya was thinking. Do people have to physically come to a place? Sometimes one comes to one's old home in thoughts, in spirit.

For a moment, she wanted to tell the father in Ishan that his lost child had come this evening, but she remained silent.

Ishan said: I don't know what I was thinking, why I opened up Lavi's things today. I will put them back tomorrow.

Aranya said cautiously: I've put everything back in the boxes.

Ah!

Whenever I open up his things, I always think whether there is any point in keeping them. But then, I gather them up again and put them safely back. Each time I touch his school uniform, it feels like he's still there in it. I know for certain that he is somewhere, even if he's not here. He was thirteen when he left, he would have become someone's father by now.

They laughed a strange laugh together, as if feeling lighter.

Ishan said: One day, just as we were leaving for a Krishnamurti talk, Lavi started insisting, 'I want to come with you'.

We tried to make him understand: 'What'll you do there. You'll just get bored sitting there.'

'I want to listen to him.'

'No, you're still too young. You won't understand him.'

'What are you saying, Ma-Papa. If I can read Einstein, I can also understand Krishnamurti's talk. A bit at least, even if not all that he says.'

'Son, you won't be able to grasp the meaning of Krishnamurti's words. There's no point in insisting.'

'Papa, let me come, just so that I can see him. I like his face a lot in the photos. Such an Indian face.'

Aranya listened to this episode, as if she already knew the child.

The mist of the past lifted and dispersed.

It felt good that you came in this weather. It was a bit awkward at first. Lavi's things were lying around, and I was feeling old and spent, as if the bundle of past had burst open and spilt over.

Aranya's face hardened. Then she spoke warmly: Everything's become so old. The paper is parched and cracking. What's the use of going through such old stuff anew?

Yes, you're right.

It had begun to rain again. They talked. It felt like they were in the mountains.

When the rain patters so incessantly on tin roofs, I feel quite enchanted by the Almighty.

Ishan laughed.

I find it fascinating, the way clouds thunder and lightening flashes. But I begin to regard the Almighty with doubt and dismay when rivers break their banks and sweep away villages, towns, houses, farms and cattle; like other ordinances, the Lord of the Universe also resorts to acts of terror. He motions his divine managerial team to cause destruction. Intimidate them, strike fear in them. Only then will they learn to improve—

fold their hands and bow in devotion. This is the policy the self-appointed Almighty follows.

Ishan looked on, saying nothing.

Aranya smiled, but Ishan looked grave. He looked at her for a while, then asked: Are you not a believer?

Who can say, I am not one. How can I compare my belief to anyone else's? There must be some part of Him in me.

Ishan got up and switched on the radio. If you want to hear the commotion on TV …

No. Radio is fine …

After they heard the news, they talked for a long time.

Ishan was talking about Almora. Almora, Kalimath, Mirtola, Himavati Cottage. Earl Brewster and his wife Elisabeth. Earl and Elisabeth were both painters. Earl used to paint mountain peaks. Snow held a strange fascination for him. Shunyata had presented me with a painting.

Brewster and Elisabeth were friends of D.H. Lawrence and Frieda. They had met them in Capri. They had been on board the same ship from Capri to Colombo.

There was another impressive American there, the Christian missionary Steiner, who was working with the Bhotias in Dharachul.

Earl Brewster used to say that Lawrence was interested in Shiva's anthropomorphic form. In those days, Earl was deeply influenced by Aurobindo's *The Life Divine*.

I had also met another extraordinary woman there—Lizzy Raymond. Her husband worked for UNESCO. Liz was writing a book on Sharada Ma.

Aranya said: My father wanted me to translate Sharada

Ma's writings into Hindi. It was Swami Ranganathan who had suggested it.

Did you do it?

No, I had no talent for translation.

I recall an unforgettable evening. We had reached Mirtola on foot, along with Shunyata. We met Krishna Prem there. Krishna Prem used to be known as Professor Nixon. He was the youngest professor of English at Lucknow University. Yashoda, the wife of another Lucknow professor, Chakravarti, was a Krishna devotee. Nixon was so impressed with her that he abandoned everything and moved with her to Mirtola.

I remember, there was a Bengali scholar, Anirban, who lived in Almora's Himavati Cottage. He was translating the Vedas into Bengali. There was also another gentleman, Boshi Sen. He was a pupil of Jagdishchandra Bose.

You could only call it a strange coincidence—for there to be, at one time, in one place, so much brilliance of so many kinds from so many places. It was an extraordinary experience.

It must have been.

Aranya began to reflect on her own experiences.

I have trekked from Kathgodam to Kausani. I'll never forget the trek from Ramgarh to Mukteshwar, especially the steep climb from Nathuakhan to Mukteshwar. There were two coolies with us, towing our baggage. As we climbed higher from Sitala Estate, sweat dripped in beads from head to foot. Climbing was no problem for me in those days, but coming down steep slopes was difficult. You'd think if you ran down at great speed, you didn't feel tired. But as our feet grow older, they shrink from running.

It was as if Aranya was gazing at Mukteshwar.

Ishan searched Aranya's face, then briefly closed his eyes and said: I have more to say. Do you feel like listening?

Aranya nodded.

I was on probation then and posted in Almora. One day I went to Shunyata's house to give him his mail and some stamps.He was a Danish citizen. Ramana Maharishi had given him that name when he saw the silence of his gaze. I could see that he was happy I had come. He gave me tea. He was saying so much to me with his silence. Whatever he said reached me, wordlessly, knocking on the door of my inner self. His cottage seemed like a dream, painted against a vast landscape. As we sat outside, evening fell upon us. I made to get up, but Shunyata motioned to me to sit down. And then, looking at the mountain peaks, he said:

How the snow changes colour.

Slowly, the evening darkened. The pure blue of the sky was adorned by the moon. The world appeared to be extraordinary, rare, and being born a human in this world more so.

It's impossible to say how long we kept sitting there. The long evening felt like an aeon. A completeness that cannot be repeated. I can see it even today. The canopy of the pure blue sky, stars, mountains, their faraway peaks deepening, darkening. Everything so translucent, as if the self could see the self. Shunyata looked magnificent as he came out holding two cups. Still as the mountain peaks, swift as the winds.

I couldn't fathom then what was happening to me. I knew just enough to sense that it was special. I still feel that specialness. Whatever is mine today is the gift of that evening.

We were startled into awareness at the same time. We stood stock still at the cottage gate. It was a moment of self-churning.

Shunyata's eyes seemed to be reading my mind.

Softly but distinctly, he had said: All of us have to reach the source of our own being. We'll reach it. I won't keep you any longer. Go now. Shunyata smiled, as if giving leave to a child.

Ishan sat silently for a long time, as if still connected to that moment.

Shunyata's laughter, in the stillness of the mountains, seemed like the pure, undeterred flow of a waterfall. Somewhat like the crazy boy you met on that road in Darjeeling.

Aranya, that laughter was like a kernel of procreative power coming to life in that moment.

It was deeply personal, pure, and hidden, and after all these years, as subtle as it was then. It makes me happy that I lived that extraordinary moment. Something unfurled in that moment, something that was concealed in it.

After I was transferred from Almora, I continued to write to Shunyata. He would respond with long letters. I used to send him stamps of upto five rupees; we had decided that limit together, and I didn't have the right to cross that line.

He once wrote to me: 'Ishan, you exist not only in yourself, but also in me. I am your permanent address, am I not? I feel your presence in my being. Do you know why? It's the purity of your being. Remember then, that you are truly Ishan, not only in name, but also for Shunyata. The purity of this relationship, this existence, will need to be protected.'

Aranya was startled. Ancient Hindu thought!

Ishan, how old are you?

Oh, twenty-five, twenty-six.

Aranya smiled mischievously.

He said: There'll come a time when you'll understand the meaning of Shunyata's words. He said, ever so often, you can't become a complete man without having learnt to love like a woman.

Ishan watched for a reaction on Aranya's face.

Waah! Women would like to learn to love like men. As much as is absolutely necessary. Not so that they dissolve into their attachment.

They looked at each other for a long time. Then suddenly, Aranya laughed. Two minds in the Universe, a woman's and a man's, looking at one point but from different directions. Looking to see that, as human beings, they attain similar rights—looking so that they may be able to live and experience them.

two

I want the shades of red and yellow to colour my sorrow.

Who was it, who said that memory fades in its own time, even if you can retrace your feet back in age. The only way out is to slip out of the grip of numbers. And yes, the red and yellow words don't come from the mouths of saints and mahatmas. They come from the one who painted his inadequacies in living colours as he left. Who painted the warmth of the afternoon with his brush before his departure. So that he could rise again each time he was defeated. Why does time knock him out so often? Perhaps so that he can spring to his feet again? A deprivation, bad stars, and a desert reaching out into the distance. Van Gogh! A vivid warmth flowing out from the colours soaking the brush. Sunflowers!

Whatever you lost and found, Aranya, was not so filled with despair, after all. Something continued to sparkle, even if erratically. Something continued to light up the darkness around you.

Dusk declines and becomes night by the force of its own being. Night becomes old and renews itself as morning. Each moment is on the wings of change. At times the sharp edges of your inside cut into something, at other times they leave behind scars, and sometimes there come tears, filtered through drops of blood. We are always being transformed, chance and coincidence fastened to memory, season after season. The mind doesn't let go of what ceases to be; it fastens itself to old links in the chain. Then it returns, reviews them, and then, turns them around again.

That evening at Ishan's was like the crackle of a page when you go through an old novel, parched so yellow with age that it wouldn't really matter if you deciphered the year of its publication.

Almost a week later, Aranya invited Ishan over for tea. So easily, that there was no question of formality.

She asked over the phone: Have you had tea?

No, just about to put the water to boil.

How about my place today? I'm about to make tea too.

You won't need lemons?

No, I have some in the fridge.

Aranya put the tea tray on the table, and with it; nuts and low-sugar biscuits.

Ishan arrived with a tin of honey and neem leaves: I plucked them on my morning walk today. They're washed and dried. You can keep them in the fridge if you like.

Thanks, Ishan. I like chewing them.

I am surprised that you don't mind the taste of neem.

I eat both things, sweet and bitter, with equal relish. You can guess that from my speech. It's not just sweet.

She laughed.

To truly get the taste of sweets, you need to keep eating neem and bitter gourd.

Surely not because of diabetes?

No, that hasn't shown up in any check-up yet. But there's no way of knowing what'll happen next. Any kind of mischief is possible in ancient bodies.

Ishan picked up the biscuits, pushing aside the cashew nuts.

It's good to beware of cashew. It has high cholesterol content. I heard an interesting story the other day. If the boss is getting in the way of your promotion, get him to eat cashew nuts to his heart's content. He'll take leave of you forever and you'll get the hike you want.

They laughed for a long time.

Aranya lifted the tea-cosy off the tea-pot.

No, let the tea steep longer. In the meantime, I'll read out some lines to you. I came across them in a file, so I brought them over. I thought you'd like them. We were talking about Shunyata that evening, weren't we? This is an excerpt from a letter of his:

'I am blessed that I stand on the brilliant white of the Himalayas. It's like a dream. This moment is dedicated to all that exists. This moment, this day, this afternoon. A helicopter flies above, the banners of its sound-waves flutter in the air. Drops of water snap off icy mountains and turn into rivers. The sun blazes in the blue sky above. I stand below on my two feet, speechless and full of gratitude.

'Oh, beloved God of sunshine, keep showering mankind with your wealth.'

The moist loftiness of the words lingered in the room. They pleased Aranya and touched her heart.

For a moment I felt as if I was standing high up on Khardung

La Pass and saying these lines. Someday, I'll read out what I've written to you. Was this piece written originally in English?

Yes, Aranya. I translated it into Hindi.

The Himalayas are eternal for us Indians. Their story is the story of our nation. They overwhelm rather than terrify us. Even though he is Danish, Shunyata has painted the scene with our sensibility. The Himalayas are a sanskara, deeply ingrained in us.

Aranya spoke: By the way, I plan to send a notice to the Municipality right away, asking them to pay some attention to our ancient lungs. The city's smog is blackening our souls.

How is your work going?

Sometimes I work so fast that I feel I'm far ahead of everyone else. At other times, I am so slow that I feel I lag far behind. I specialize in eccentricity.

At this turn in our age, one should expect to discipline oneself.

You're right. But no such trait binds me to my nature. When afternoon wears off...

You give the impression of being in top form still. You seem to have tons of energy.

The essence of my existence is contained in me. That's why I seem so, perhaps.

No, we ignore our history so that our virtues and vices can repeat themselves. Careless about the past at times and anxious for the future.

And sometimes we forget all this and drop into an oblivious slumber. Speaking for myself, my sleep in the mornings is so deep, it's as if I cease to exist.

It's not good to sleep so late into the morning.

I know that, but it's not easy to change habits that are decades-old.

Ishan said: Asanas and exercise keep the body alert. The arteries begin to narrow when one reaches this shore of life. They slacken, so some kind of movement becomes essential. And more than anything, the daily walk.

I know the difference between dawn and dusk. Time is part old, part new. Old shapes seem new and new ones seem old, as if I've known them forever.

They appear in dreams, unfamiliar shapes. They disappear when I try to tell them apart. Yes, sometimes I see blue water flowing through rocks.

Sometimes, in my sleep I see it's a dream, and also that it's not a dream, and that I stand there looking at someone as if I were that person. There's a person out there who is me.

Interesting!

Aranya looked at Ishan. Who is it who looks and who is it who is looked at?

It's not quite what you mean, but when I sleep, I see long rows of laburnum, yellow blossoms and green fruit dangling from their boughs. I feel like a tree myself, covered in yellow and green. I used to walk on the blazing, beautiful Hailey Road in the mornings and evenings. Perhaps that's lurking somewhere in my mind.

Ishan looked at Aranya's ageing face.

It may be past now, but just see where we land if we try replicating it.

When you absorb the core of someone else's gaze, your own eyes get alienated from you. The meaning of my being lies for me within myself. That's what limits it, perhaps. My being is a necessity for myself, because I am alone.

Ishan was silent, trying to gauge the significance of her words.

Aranya was searching for Ishan's reaction to the words she had spoken.

Fresh tea was brewed and had.

You aren't going out of Delhi in the next few days, are you?

I have no plans at the moment.

I am going away for a whole month.

Aranya urged him on:That's good. Going away every now and then cures the boredom born of the monotony of a city. I have travelled a lot in the past, but it's a bother now.

Because of having to make all those preparations?

It upsets my routine.

It's the other way round for me. I feel a new thrill each time I think of going away. My suitcase is always ready for travel.

I know. Not one, but three.

How come you know that?

I've seen you a couple of times, carrying them from the taxi to the lift. I've wanted to help, but I have strict instructions from my doctor about lifting weight, on account of my eyes.

I am an old-fashioned railway traveller. My whole household moves with me.

Ishan became serious. It's time to lighten the baggage now.

Aranya said mischievously. Shifting house twice or thrice has halved my baggage.

Ishan looked at her in response, as if to say, 'I was saying something else'.

I'm going to put you to some trouble. I have a friend whom I entrust with such work but he's away on a tour, so I am leaving this envelope with you.

Are they telephone, electricity bills?

No, I've had those paid. But anything can happen anywhere, and quite suddenly. It could also be on a holiday. I don't want people to have to upset their arrangements because of me. That wouldn't be right.

What makes you think like that, Ishan? You can leave without getting anxious. Nothing's going to happen.

It's not to be taken lightly, Aranya. My friend Malware found eternal rest at London airport on his way back from America. Mrs Malware was with him. She did all the running around and informed the children. Kaushik and Alka could also get to London. You've met them, haven't you?

I have. But why can't we regard this episode as an exception?

Ishan replied calmly. Because we're standing in the queue of those who could be called up any time. Leaving is also a process.

Even if you weren't to add that last bit, all of us are destined to go one day. It doesn't help to worry about it before that.

I understand that. But don't forget, I'm alone. There's no one before or after me. That's why I've come to hand this to you.

Forgive me, I said this because you look like an older youth to me.

The same as you. We were born on the same day.

That's surprising. How did you find out?

Some people can find out things from anywhere at all.

But I have some objection to that, my friend. In the years ahead, I plan to reduce my age. And please remember, I'm not your age, I'm younger. It's likely there's a mix-up with the dates of birth.

They laughed.

I'm leaving by the morning flight. We'll argue about this when I get back. I've left both cheques and cash in the envelope, and a copy of my will.

Aranya chose her words carefully. It's safe with me. Let me know when you're coming back so that I can wait for you. And in return for this, treat me to tea in a restaurant.

Then hesitatingly, she said: This is something you need to hand over to a lawyer when you come back.

You're right. But he's away at the moment. And since there's no one in my family, I felt compelled to ask you.

Ishan's words reined in Aranya's lightness. She said anxiously. I also have to do something. Then, as if some decisive moment descended upon her, she said: Perhaps the date of our departure will also be the same.

Suggest something else which could also be the same.

My mother's name was Durga. And yours?

Durga. But our fathers' names have to be different, otherwise our identities could get mixed up. Not here, up there.

Both laughed heartily.

I'll leave early in the morning, at four-thirty. Bahadur is on leave, so I am thinking if I should leave the key with you. Will it be a bother for you to wake up so early?

No, I don't go to sleep until then. I usually drink tea at that time.

Ishan said, gravely: It's important to do things in the normal way. A night's sleep is most important for the human body. The digestive system doesn't function well without it.

The better part of life is over now. We'll think about it if we are born again. How good it would have been to be born a couple of years later. We could have enjoyed the next century as well.

They looked at each other as if they were back to being young again. As if they were saying to themselves: Yes, yes, it could well happen.

three

After a week, she received a letter.

Dear Aranya,

The pigeon feed must be over by now. You have the house keys, so I'll have to bother you with this again. There are some clay bowls in the balcony. Could you fill them with millet grains and water? Also, there is a hose near the kitchen window. I would be so grateful if you watered the plants.

Ishan

After ten days, another letter.

Dear Aranya,

I had a mind to come back earlier, but for some reason I stayed on. I request you once more to take care of the pigeons.

I am sending you a card made by my friend. I hope you like it. He is over eighty, and keeps himself busy with something or the other. When I went to meet him, he was sitting on a divan, pasting leaves on cards with such care that it seemed as if it was solitude that made for such completeness. You must also know this sense of fulfillment. He offered the card to me when he was done; the serrated leaves of the Morpankhi nearly smiled at me.

He gave me with two cards—one is for you.

I hope you are well and in good spirits.

Ishan

Aranya bought millet from the bazaar in the evening, opened Ishan's flat and put it in the bowls. She attached the hose to the tap and watered the plants. The rubber plant was green, as were the long green leaves of the Vidya.

She cooked here and there. There was no clutter in the house, just sparseness. As if it was life that was being lived, not its comforts. She glanced at the shelf. Krishnamurti was there. No, no shadow of grief anywhere. Birds were chirping. The solitude of lone houses, how different it was from the fully occupied. Spare, but elegant, and ticking with the clock.

And alone.

Entirely alone.

I'm familiar with this, aren't I? That's why I can see it.

Aranya took the boarding pass in her hand and stood up from her chair. With the announcement, countless units, stationary till now, became mobile. Brisk steps forward, bags swinging from shoulders, boarding pass in hand. Passengers travelling by flight number IC 434 from Bhubaneshwar via Bhopal to Delhi are requested to proceed to gate number two.

The ceaselessness of airports. The magic of arrivals and departures. They come, they go—check-in, security, lounge-wait, and then board. Travellers … travel … each day, each morning, each night. No time is odd here. Whether the sun rises or sets, whether it is the bright half of the moon or the dark, flights continue to scale the skies, they continue to land. The airports of the world are abuzz night and day. A big comfort, that these flight concessions are also available to us seniors. And we obtain these in just two days! Isn't that astonishing.

The unfamiliar face at the Connaught Place airlines office came back to her. He had wished her well as he handed over the card to her. Given her date of birth, he must have surely conjectured how much longer the concession card would be used. This is a category of traveller whose rebated flights depend on luck alone.

The flight was three hours late. It would land in Palam Airport at midnight. From there, it would take her another hour to get home.

She had been away for fifteen days, and she hadn't left the keys with anyone to get the place cleaned. She had wanted to leave them with Ishan, but when she went to meet him she had found only Bahadur at home.

Is Sahib there?

No. He's coming back by tomorrow's flight. Can I help with anything?

Oh no, thanks.

Aranya allowed the keys to remain in her purse. One can sleep on the sofa even if the house hasn't been cleaned. A little carelessness and everything can be cleaned out, including the owner. Trying to get rid of Delhi's dust can turn out to be very costly. Looking out of the window, she saw an endless expanse of darkness. A wing of the airplane could be seen, gathering up the distances, sprinting across the skys at an uncanny pace and with poise. Stars sparkled in the spaces in between; there were so many of them that each person on Earth could claim one as theirs.

The Almighty is the bookkeeper of this world. He is in charge of arrivals and departures.

Aranya leafed through magazines for a while and then closed her eyes. Would there be anything at home after this two-week long absence? Yes, a cup of tea. Tea, powdered milk, biscuits.

The magnificent temple at Konark rose before her eyes. The satisfaction and pleasure of having seen it returned. She recalled the interesting syntax used by the old guide—Look, while the wife is inside, another woman waits outside for him. Even as the husband makes a sign to her, the wife chants a hymn of disaffection, her litany of hate.

Aranya laughed to herself. After the temple, the guide had shown her the little garden where people could rest or relax.

The scene before her closed eyes changed. Ocean, waves, and the shore held in place by wet sand!

A wave came, collected her shoe and departed.

She had stood there for a long time, waiting for it to come back.

What's this!

She saw a strong, powerful hand being laid on her purse. Just the hand! Where was the face? She screamed: who are you?!

She woke up with a start and found her own hand tightly clutching the handle of her bag.

Wandering around the whole day and waiting for the

evening flight had exhausted her. Maybe that's what was making her weary and tense.

Aranya opened her purse and checked everything. She rearranged everything—transferred the envelope with the cash from the large to the smaller, inner compartment; opened the big zipper inside and kept some change there; kept the bigger notes, held in reserve, in the secret inner pocket. Then to reassure herself, she examined her face in the compact mirror and arranged her hair, looking for the reason for her restlessness. Everything had gone well. People were pleased—Somya, his wife, the community of progressive thinkers in Bhubaneshwar. A soft breeze had enveloped her after the ceremony. The occasion had gone the way she had wanted it to. But now, long forgotten old memories had surfaced and begun to hurt.

A faceless silhouette began to slink around inside her. She fixed her eyes on something outside the window.

The sky, spread who knows how wide, expresses itself in sunshine during the day, and then stealing into the night, deepens the mystery of solitude.

Our concessional flight heads towards its rebated target. The air-hostess's voice fills the aircraft. In a short while, we shall be descending on Palam Airport. Please fasten your seat belts. Passengers are requested not to open the overhead compartments. We hope you had a pleasant flight. The temperature outside is eight degrees Celsius.

The plane came to an unhurried halt on the runway. The queue of passengers in the aisle descended slowly.

An attractive and enthusiastic air-hostess folded her hands, smiled, and said 'namaskar'. Good night.

Once on the ground, Aranya crossed the passageway quickly and pulled a trolley. With her hand resting on it, she waited for the baggage to arrive. She piled her suitcase and bag on it, got the coupon for a prepaid taxi, and pushed the trolley outside.

There was an extra attentiveness in her movements and alertness in her eyes. She had the suitcase and bag deposited in the dickey and sat in the car, the purse hanging from her shoulder.

The street seemed long, at once familiar and unfamiliar. Such was the excitement of coming back home each time she returned from a journey.

It used to be such a pleasure drinking tea at Safdarjung Airport. Cup in hand, planes taking off just ahead of us, showing prospective flyers how to fly. How long ago it seems now. Those days, those seasons, where did they disappear? And the fresh decades of youth? Aranya scolded herself. Do you really not know that those days got lost somewhere in the geography of this city?

For so many years, she's been returning home from the station or the airport and moulding herself and the house in the mode suited for travel.

Days of struggle, big and small, taking shape. Days of living through desires and their limits. Days of youth and excitement, and bearing up to the rough and tangle of days. Of expanding financial responsibilities and capabilities. Sometimes, the one tipped higher and sometimes, the other.

The clock would strike five and the headaches of office would be shut away in the drawer for the next day.

Friendships would measure the roads; the destination was Connaught Place. Those bubbly, beautiful days, of picking restaurants. Standard, Gaylord, Volga, Embassy, La

Bohéme, Nirula's, York, Ginza, Alps, Maidens. Towards the end of the month, the Coffee House or the Tea House. A cycle of spending and cutting back. Where is the better band, where do pineapple and Jungle Delight pastries taste better, and where the cheese balls and paneer pakoras? Where do we get the better sandwiches and fried fish? Wengers' cold drink Midnight Beauty and Dusty Road ice cream of Milk Bar at Scindia House. Heady days of youth …

The Sunday meeting would convene at eleven for coffee and stretch upto lunch, evening show cinema tickets tucked in pockets. Plans would be made with taste, depending on the salary at disposal. Neither a whit less nor a whit more. New Delhi's salaried class and its mores, caught in a tussle with each other. A glance always fixed on the metre of expenses and small and big wishes respected accordingly.

For years, Delhi, new and old, kept up its grandeur at all costs. With Independence, the capital began to overflow with community after aggressive community of the displaced. Here, there, everywhere. In every district of the city. The inhabitants of Delhi were plagued by belligerent refugees uprooted from villages, qasbas and towns. Duststorms swept over Delhi's culture and tastes.

And in the twinkling of an eye, pavement stalls invaded and conquered the inside of shops. As a result, the older proprietors of the shops advanced towards New Delhi.

The trams and their tracks vanished from the streets in a wink. The row of trees lining Chandni Chowk were chopped. Stoves were lit on the pavements and dal and rotis began to be made there. The Lahore Gate of the Red Fort looked on in silence. As did the residents of Delhi. Parts of the wall encircling the city were swept away. The gardens on the outskirts of Old Delhi were rapidly sold off and, in no time, disappeared into the master plan. Villages underwent a complete metamorphosis. Three hundred and four villages of Delhi district were transformed into bigger settlements. Their identities were preserved in the names of streets and small shops. And like them, we, young citizens of yesteryears, were transformed into the senior citizens of today.

That's the odd thing about the pace of time. We were insiders till the time we were in the running, and we stand outside now that we have slowed down. Entirely outside. As if travelling in a hired cab, we course through the streets of new time and yet we don't belong to it.

Ancient us in new times.

Quiet! Why think of old times and feel dejected. Keep away from that.

She glanced outside. The streets glistened with rows of light. At one time, this Kitchener Hostel area used to be deserted. Now it wallows in quiet luxury and in the subdued hum of embassies. She looked at the driver and cleaner in the front seats of her taxi. After ten in the night, the driver needs the cleaner. He may feel threatened by the passengers seated behind him. There is no danger to the lone passenger, though; the taxi is pre-paid. She looked at her watch. Twelve-twenty. At least another twenty minutes to get home. The car was descending rapidly from the incline of an over-bridge in the fascinating but strangely frightening stillness of the winter night.

Suddenly the driver braked. As if he had stopped at someone's command.

Aranya asked: What happened, Driver Sahib?

Someone was knocking on the back window.

Before Aranya could think further, the driver stretched his arm back and lowered the pane.

Show your baggage. Hand over your purse.

Who are you?

Police.

Please show your identity card.

You want to know my identity, madam? Shall I snap it open and show it to you?

The knife glistened in his hand. You know what this is, don't you?

Yes, but I've nothing worth searching.

Stop arguing.

The tightly clutched purse was snatched away by a tight fist.

Open the dickey! The voice cracked like a whip.

The cleaner scrambled out quickly and opened the dickey.

The baggage was lifted out and the door slammed.

Go drop this old hen home! She won't get there if she stops by the police station on the way.

The car started.

The sentry's shadow still loomed large.

The driver turned his head and said: They were in uniform, but they weren't real policemen.

When they turned the next bend, Aranya said: Driver Sahib, this is a pre-paid taxi, isn't it?

Madam, what could we have done? What can we do if looters in police uniform stop us? You saw the knife, didn't you? What if we lost our lives?

Hand-in-glove.

You stopped the car when they gave a signal, didn't you?

What else could we do in a situation like that, madam?

If you hadn't stopped, how could they have followed us? They were on foot.

Not at all, a car was parked a few steps away.

Madam, it's true you've lost your luggage, but nothing really bad happened to you. The mischief they can get up to. Was there a lot of expensive stuff in your baggage? Camera, jewellery?

Stop this nonsense and take the car to the police station.

We'll drop you near the police station. We're not getting involved in this. This is our work time.

You'll have to go.

Then the driver spoke with some empathy: Madam, you'll freeze at the police station. If you try to get someone on the phone, you'll find the line isn't working. You'll get nothing from the police station. In a situation like this, it's best for a passenger like you to get home safely.

The sound of a bullet pierced Aranya's ears, as if shot off from her own chest. If only I had a gun... But I don't.

He changed lanes.

She looked outside.

The car was moving in the direction of her house.

If only a Flying Squad would come by at this moment.

The guard at the gate signalled them to stop. He lifted the register.

Aranya told the driver: Stop the car here.

Sahib, you'll have trouble carrying the baggage to the lift.

There is no baggage.

Reaching inside, she drew a long breath.

The house keys were in her purse.

Perplexed, she stood there for a while, then moved towards the lift in the next block.

There was no option but to ring Ishan's bell.

It's past one now.

Somewhere else?

No, this is not the time to go anywhere else either.

She rang the doorbell.

It rang for a long time.

The door opened.

At this hour!

Perplexity and coldness in Ishan's voice. In his eyes, a kind of drowsy awkwardness.

It's past one. Was your flight late?

Yes.

Where's your baggage?

Something happened. We'll talk tomorrow. But I'll have to stay here. I don't have my house keys. That's why I'm here …

Ishan looked alarmed, but he remained silent.

After a moment, he said: There's fresh linen in the guestroom. It was the washerman's day today. The duvet is thin; you'll need another blanket.

Ishan went to his room. She heard the sound of a cupboard opening. A blanket was placed on the sofa.

Good, I heard the bell. There's some fruit in the fridge. You can make tea if you like. You'll find milk, sugar, everything you need, on the shelf.

Thanks. Good night.

Good night.

A tray on the dining table. Two glasses. Lemons. Honey. A flask, a knife, a spoon.

The start of a new day.

Aranya stood for a while in the dining room.

No purse. No keys. If she had given the keys to Bahadur, she could have slept the night in her own flat. She had doubted Bahadur's reliability. That's what comes of being unnecessarily suspicious. Did you think that someone like Bahadur would spirit away your flat? No. It was just looking out for your safety. Who knows, perhaps when they have rifled through my luggage, some of it will turn up again. At one time, there used to be a box at the General Post Office where pickpockets would drop off the empty shells of stolen purses, passports, keys. Beyond pens, watches or cash, they weren't really interested in troubling people by keeping their stuff. Would this courteous gesture have survived the ravages of time?

Are you still lost and wandering? These were not pickpockets; they were robbers. She could have phoned Kaul Sahib. At that time!

No, it's one-thirty now.

She opened her eyes after a light morning nap.

She switched on the lamp.

Four-thirty.

Go to sleep.

She turned on the other side and plunged into a deep slumber again. It was the exhaustion of losing her baggage.

She stretched her hands, as if to collect something and returned empty-handed again. Where will my clothes be? Perhaps in the second-hand bazaar. No, not this week, not so soon. Not necessarily in this city. It'll take time. Who'll wear them?

She went to the bathroom and washed her face and hands several times, as if she needed to wash off the pollution of the past hours. The satisfaction of touching a fresh towel... Of feeling fresh.

She made tea in the kitchen and began to feel like herself again as she sipped it. That dream was a taste of what was to come. The same strong hand on my purse, reaching for me. I should have gone to the police station, I should have had it reported. But there was no scope for that. If I had a pocket torch, I could have at least caught a glimpse of the faces of those uniformed men. The driver and cleaner were party to it.

Perhaps I can look for my clothes in the Sunday bazaar. That's where they'll be sold. Right there on the pavement. On the other hand, the brothers would have been disappointed on opening the suitcase. Three pairs of clothes. A shawl, a jersey, two files in the bag, and just a thousand in the purse. And the rebate card for senior citizens.

You're forgetting the keys. That's your biggest headache! That's not safe. You'll need to get the lock changed. The running around, apart from the expense involved...

She gave a start as she saw a shadow behind the window pane. It's the breeze. The abundance and the poverty of life showing up at once. Be quiet! This is hardly the time to unveil secrets.

Look for the tumult in the silence within yourself. That's where you'll find your story.

Maybe, but I feel a deep satisfaction with myself, quite apart from any relationship or friendship.

Then why do you call out to those deep within, those who lie in ambush waiting for you?

There are several editions of me. They can't be seen all the time. But when they resurface, they take aim at me with lost weapons.

Perhaps some enemy.

No, sometimes friendships with opposites don't call forth friendship.

And Ishan.

An intense, aware relationship.

How come I saw that hand! I was in the air. Not on the ground.

Her feet felt warm. Sticking her legs out of the blanket, she covered herself up to the neck.

A room exactly the same as in her own flat. The same map, the same size, the same shape ... but new all the same.

What's new about it?

Try and take it easy now.

Leave the taxi incident behind you. The voices of the night, woven out of dark, subtle, sounds. The car starting. The brake of the car as it came inside the gate, the noise of the guard's shoes ...

The deep grey stillness of Ishan's guestroom. A stillness distinct from her own place in its clarity. Who knows what the dense, deeply knotted grey of her flat has absorbed in itself.

We are so different, the two of us.

Everything in my house is detached from itself, free from routine, while everything in his is in the grip of discipline, order and system.

A dusky light suffused the room as she opened her eyes. The key dangling from the door consoled her. Mine has been lost, but I can still see this one.

Ishan is humming something—reciting ancient *Saundaryalahri* verses. How different this is from the beginning of my day.

> May we be blessed
> by the streak of vermillion parting your dark hair
> breaking loose from its bond of hostile tresses,
> flowing from your beautiful forehead
> like the ray of the morning sun.

I bow to Shri's dance of creation
in concert with the nine rasas of Shiva's dance of destruction
emanating compassion, enabling existence
I acknowledge in you Lord of the World, father and mother.

The hymn to Durga resounded through the stillness of the morning. With her head resting on the pillow, Aranya thought of her usual craving for a cup of tea and smiled. But for that, no other daily ritual for you.

We belong to two different species, jatis. Those with rites and those without rites.

In that comfortable haze, she sensed some activity, following which, the front door clicked shut. Ishan left for his morning walk.

She'll need to wait till he comes back.

As she lay there, her gaze wandered to the key again. I could open this door, go out and try opening the door of my own guestroom with this key. It won't work, of course, if it is bolted from the inside.

Aranya stood up. She made the bed and pulled the bedcover over it. Folding the blanket, she placed it at the foot of the bed. Then she took the key to Ishan's guestroom and, locking his flat, went across to her own. She turned the key in the door of her guestroom, which had a separate entrance, and it opened.

A long sigh of relief.

She took out the key, turned it into her side of the keyhole and let it hang there.

Keys get snatched. They get lost. And then, somewhere or the other, they turn up again.

She shook out the cover of the diwan, doubled the pillow, and pulled the duvet over herself. The fragrance of her own house rose from the bed linen, and she fell asleep.

Home.

four

Hello.

Ishan was on the phone.

We haven't met for quite a while. I knew you were busy, so I felt I shouldn't disturb you. How are you?

I am well. Aranya laughed. I eat turmeric with my milk, just as you told me.

Really! Have you been doing it all these days?

No, not quite, but lately, eating green turmeric has become an important part of my daily routine.

Waah! But have you forgotten about everything else?

Not at all. First you peel the turmeric and grind it. Put it in a cup. Add the milk. A spoon of honey to top it off. The bottle cap needs to be opened, too. Only then can the spoon reach the mouth. A mercy that it doesn't have to be ground in the pestle.

You're very lazy, it seems.

Yes, indeed.

Half the pleasure of food lies in its preparation.

I'm sure. But I stay far from it.

I like doing everything with my own hands; it gives me great pleasure.

You're truly modern. Otherwise, like ancient Indian householders, you'd leave all the work to someone else. You can keep your status only if you have ten pairs of hands working for you.

Too much tea isn't good for your health.

Why don't we drink to each other's health with turmeric milk!

They laughed for a long time.

Ishan reminded her. Your telephone bill has arrived, hasn't it? If you haven't paid it yet, leave a signed check in my mailbox. I have to go pay mine tomorrow.

Many thanks, Ishan. That'll save me a *big* headache.

Does it really need such a huge adjective?

As long as my carelessness continues, yes. The bills arrive; I see them and put them away carefully so that I don't forget them. Then I forget them, and later I have to queue up to get another copy.

Tag it and stick it on a wall. If it stays in front of you, you'll remember it.

I'll try that out.

Have you had breakfast?

Not yet.

It's already eleven. It's important to take breakfast seriously.

You're right, but it's far too late now for me to get rid of my bad habits.

Aranya was out buying fruit in the evening. Ishan showed up just as she was ready to leave.

He picked oranges, limes and chikoos.

I'm buying some for you as well.

By all means. Aranya offered him paper bags. I've also

bought pomegranates in two separate bags. One for you and one for myself.

Thanks, Aranya. I'm not simply returning a favour, it looks like we think alike. Our dates correspond, don't they?

Aranya said mischievously: Not dates, just one date—the date of birth.

We'll take it as an effect of that, then.

Aranya couldn't help joking when she saw Ishan's hands full with bags of fruit: Bapu said, buying fruit with a free hand means true saving.

As they walked to the gate, Ishan said: I'd like to go and see Kishore. He's just come back from the nursing home. Will you come along? He will like it.

She felt anxious all of a sudden. The end of the journey.

What if we went there after tea? Why don't we go to my place and dump these bags there? I have some fresh murmuras. I just have to switch on the kettle.

Seeing Aranya immersed in thought, Ishan said: There's some sandesh at my place. I know you like them.

He opened the door, went into the kitchen, washed and dried the fruit, put them in the fridge and brought tea to the table.

That was fast!

Just let it brew some more. In the meantime, let's phone Mrs Kishore.

This is Ishan speaking. How is Kishore? We could come meet him, if you think it won't inconvenience him? And yes, Aranya is also here. How would it be if she also came along?

Certainly, do come. He'll be glad to see you both. For some reason, he's taken to just lying there silently.

We'll start in ten minutes.

Aranya was making a second cup of tea for herself.

So much hot tea isn't good for you. It harms the liver and the teeth. It must also make other old ailments crop up again. Health culture has developed enormously. I've been reading a lot on it lately. I could give you some good books.

I know relatively little about these things.

It'll be good to boost your knowledge now. You can cure some minor and even major ailments without the help of a doctor.

I'll go put something warm on. Will be back in a couple of minutes.

Draping a shawl around herself, she climbed down the stairs. She looked at her watch and, in rapid strides, reached the flower-seller. Bright flowers covered the pavement. If only flowers could speak, would they allow themselves to be sold like this? To be sold. Without uttering a word. Mutely. Perhaps not. They would object to our excesses.

Bouquet of flowers in hand, Aranya almost ran back.

Ishan was walking in her direction. He signalled his silent approval to her on seeing the flowers.

They found Mrs Kishore seated in her drawing room. She gave a detailed account of all that had happened in the nursing home. Then lowering her voice, she said: I've bought a wheelchair, but he won't use it. He doesn't say much. Just lies there silently. He perked up a little when he heard you were coming. He got himself ready to come to the drawing room.

The male nurse stationed the wheelchair near Ishan.

Hello, Kishore! Ishan bent over him and touched his hand.

You're feeling better now, aren't you?

Aranya rose to present the flowers to him; Mrs Kishore took them and said to Kishore: They're for you.

Kishore was looking intently at Aranya as if trying to place her. And then in a voice from some unseen world, he said: How are you? Glancing at the flowers, he said: Thank you!

Mrs Kishore said: We've bought new shoes for him. One of his legs has shrunk a bit. Only physiotherapy can heal it.

Ishan leaned over to Kishore: Yes, some activity will boost your blood circulation. I've brought some books for you. There's no need to exhaust yourself. Read slowly and only as much as you can.

The old Kishore returned from somewhere: Have you finished reading them?

No, I just bought them. I thought I'd read them after you.

A deep tiredness came over Kishore again.

I can't read them now, Ishan. You read them first.

He isn't interested in anything, Ishan. Leave the books here. I'll read them out to him.

Ishan looked at Kishore: I can send you Krishnamurti's cassettes if you like.

Kishore did not say anything.

Our daughter and son-in-law have looked after him so well. The surgery was successful. The bone has healed. There's no need to be so depressed.

Kishore is going to try. It's important to get up and keep moving your foot. All right then, I'll call you.

As they moved towards the door, Aranya glanced back.

Kishore was looking neither at Ishan's and Aranya's waving hands, nor at the footsteps moving away from him. His gaze was fixed at a point far away, beyond the door.

Perhaps he was looking at his near and dear ones, carrying

him away on their shoulders, to a place from which no one returns. The last scene in this world, which one doesn't see oneself, though everyone else sees it.

What body language is that?

Someone looking for himself on that road, just before the game ends.

Aranya and Ishan climbed downstairs in silence. Neither of them spoke as they moved towards their respective lifts.

Three days later, Ishan was on the phone.

Kishore is no more. We'll have to go to Nigambodh ghat. Do you want to come?

No, Ishan, I won't go.

Ishan hung up the receiver silently.

Aranya read the manuscript, corrected some mistakes, sealed the envelope and wrote the address. New traits are manifesting themselves. Why has it begun to seem so hard to write addresses on envelopes? What could be the reason for such laziness?

Are you looking for excuses to buy a computer? Will you be able to manage the new machine? Work on it? It'll strain your eyes and neck.

The bell rang. She opened the door and handed the envelope to the courier.

Thank goodness she had taken care of this work.

She glanced at her watch—four o'clock. Lie down for an hour. Tea after that.

She picked up the book by her bedside.

The body rides on the wings of change in order to live.

With each breath, we pull in hydrogen, oxygen, carbon, nitrogen. The stomach, the heart, the lungs and the brain are engulfed in air.

The skin regenerates itself every month, also the lining of the stomach. Every five days, the liver, and in six weeks, the entire frame of the body. Even so, we feel that change is unusual, while ninety-five percent of the body's cells are being transformed, growing and continually regenerating the body.

In its subtle form, the stock of cells is connected to a powerful cosmic computer. Cosmic computer, with ultra sound signals. And the wonder, that nothing happens unexpectedly.

Our body is evidence of all the experiences we have known and lived. I am not only me. I am also all that I have assembled in myself.

Ishan's bookmark lay in the book. Aranya stood up and looked at herself in the mirror. How much had changed. How did it happen? Where did that heap of time go? Multiple decades? Time doesn't gnaw at the body; it is absorbed by the body. Along with all its dirt, mud, whirls of dust.

She asked herself suspiciously: Are you just collecting the rage of the years? No, also the pleasures and excitements. Bits of memory, not easy to return or untangle. As if all that was learnt by heart is being said in a single word, in sentences flashing with words and maxims that sparkle with meaning. The exponentiation of existence.

Do you see anything beyond this? You use the pretext of having no one to carry on after you, to devolve into yourself, into the writing of the beauty of this world, sunlight and shade, wind and water, moon and sun. How much there is to see! Aranya stretched her arms and opened the window: Keep blowing, sun-drenched winds, as long as I am alive. Keep reaching out to me. I wish my time here to be vibrant. All that bears fruit, all that is created—I wish to mark flowerbeds of words with that.

> No one is excluded from the pressure of existence.
> Fire lives off the death of Earth
> Wind, off the death of fire
> Water, off the death of wind
> And Earth is kept alive by the death of water.

Aranya pushed away the blanket covering her.

She glanced at the clock. Four-thirty. Time for tea.

She went into the kitchen, then turned back, lifted the telephone receiver and dialled Ishan's number.

Have you saved some time to waste? There seems to be little room for that in the way you manage your life.

Ishan laughed. You've wrapped up your work for the day, it seems.

I've entrusted the envelope to the courier. This evening is for relaxation, only relaxation.

Then come over, you are being invited over to tea.

Aranya perked up. Changing her clothes quickly, she felt fresh. She had just moved towards the door when the phone rang.

She decided she was not at home and let the phone ring. She cut two pieces of cake, packed some savouries and shut the box. The phone kept ringing for a long time.

The lift was not working.

She took the lift from the next block and rang Ishan's bell.

The bell rang for a long time. Then Ishan came to the door.

Didn't you see I had left the door open, Aranya?

Aranya came inside, shut the door and said gravely, We read the newspapers everyday, don't we? You can't just leave your door open like that. Whoever is at the door can wait.

If someone else were to come thundering in … You can't really ignore this, Ishan. It's dangerous.

She instinctively looked at her own hands. Oh, where is my key? Have I left it hanging at my door! I'll come right back.

Aranya went out swiftly and back to the flat the way she had come. The key was hanging from her door. As she locked the door, she decided to look inside. She checked all the rooms, both bathrooms and the kitchen. She felt lighter as she shut her door.

This time, Ishan's door was locked.

He smiled as he opened it: It's all right now, isn't it?

Yes, you have to be vigilant, day in and day out. I'm going to have a second automatic lock put on my door.

It'll be difficult if you forget your keys.

I'll keep a duplicate copy with you.

I wouldn't advise that.

Why not?

For your own convenience. Our timings don't match.

Aranya pricked up her ears.

Why not?

I rest when you work and you rest when I'm working! We'll both be inconvenienced.

I understand.

They looked at each other, fearful of some unknown intimacy that hovered between acceptance and non-acceptance.

Aranya reflected in silence.

Shall we make tea?

Two cups.

On the table, there were cake, gram, murmure and delicately made gajrela.

Help yourself.

Please, after you.

Both stirred their tea.

Stirring up a storm in the Arabian Sea?

Aranya broke into laughter.

Maybe, but that's of little use in the face of your calm Pacific gaze.

Ishan's face changed.

We're talking like adversaries.

I'm not competitive, as far as I can tell.

But competitiveness can be detected at all times in your countenance.

You can draw anything at all from an oppositional stand and confront it with your truth.

Aranya saw a glimmer of disbelief on Ishan's face.

My ignorance can also be an intimation of my mono-perspective. Please feel free to say what you want.

It is quite appropriate to develop your mental and physical capacities the way your nature and your temperament allow, but to terrorize others with it is not.

Aranya laughed out loud.

Are you saying I'm a terrorist, Ishan? I am a good, clean soul.

Ishan shook his head. It's true not only for you. We all have our own narratives of desire and passion. However, the soul remains unaffected by all that.

That's surely the case, but unlike you, I am no seer of the self.

You are self-absorbed.

Is that a negative quality?

Cerebral dispute!

Logic is the mainstay of all sciences.

Ishan's forehead puckered and then relaxed again. He took some savouries on his plate and asked: Have you read the Upanishads?

Yes and no. I've read them, but I have no interest in the complexities of the soul, of god, being and other such things. Or any kind of escapist thought …

Indian thought and philosophy are not escapist. They've studied the problems of existence through the prism of tested value systems.

It was as if both of them were laughing at each other, and yet with each other.

This seems to incite your tendency to lecture.

Let's defer this conversation.

Aranya searched Ishan's face. And then, as if making fun of herself: Thus the mystery!

Thus the Upanishads!

God cannot create another god.

In spite of all his skills, a Brahman cannot create another Brahman out of a non-Brahman. What would you say to that, Ishan?

Ishan said firmly: Nothing at all.

Do say something. I am not in the reservations quota. I can understand what matters, even if the shastras are beyond me.

Ishan laughed out loud.

Enough now. Let's change the topic. Not with politics but with tea with honey, black pepper and cinnamon. We're getting worked up about the business of living. And yes, I was forgetting tulsi.

They drank tea.

I'll be off now. I have to get isabgol husk from the shop downstairs.

Who knows what kind of boredom Aranya detected in Ishan's face as she said sweetly: Tukaram's *abhang* on the one side and the mischiefs of the stomach on the other. Discipline is necessary. The truth is that the stomach is a terrorist. It takes possession of the body at the smallest chance.

Precisely why this topic is not any the less significant. As we all know, a terrorist can accomplish any number of things. Headaches, giddiness, dry mouth, upset liver. Of course, I remain responsible. I'm an insomniac, so I am duly punished.

Aranya and Ishan laughed.

Nature has another cure for this. Gandhi regarded it as very effective. Honey and lemon. Lentil sprout. Soaked and roasted daliya.

Enough, Ishan. I don't have the patience to put all this together.

Aranya laughed. I open the tin of daliya and immediately shut it. Instead, I roast semolina and make myself shira.

I'll make daliya for you.

What do you add to it?

Munaqqa, chuhara, cardamom, cinnamon, magaz, almonds. If I make it for breakfast tomorrow, I'll bring some over to you. Otherwise, the day after.

Thanks, Ishan. I'll keep a look out for it. We'll meet again.

Ishan smiled. Aranya was speaking as if she knew there would surely be another meeting. That could be, but also not be.

five

There could also come a day when we don't find each other.

Aranya knitted her brows.

Must we hurl frustration at each other, even if in jest?

Listen, Aranya, listen.

Aranya had already left.

Ishan was coming after many weeks.

The bell rang. The door opened. Come in.

How are you?

And you?

I am well, thank you.

What's up? The house seems very silent.

The television's not on, there's no music either.

Ishan seemed to be searching for the right words for the walls enclosed in curtains.

Aranya said: We can hear the silence because we live alone.

Do you feel lonely?

No. Yet, when I come home from somewhere, I wash my hands and feet, change my clothes and make tea to welcome myself. Of course, I know that there are no other voices at home. And each sound which is not mine is made by others—who are outside. In that case, being friends with the TV is not so bad.

Does it make you anxious?

No, every experience, and what it demands of me, is something new. It keeps me occupied. I can say this with confidence that I never get bored.

The phone rang.

Some friend of Aranya's. Cursory conversation about each other's well being.

I don't know why we remain trapped in the banalities. It disturbs me every once in a while, but it also makes me laugh.

You want distant intimacies so as to avoid having to hear family grievances. Wouldn't it be good to air them sometimes?

Familial attachment and emotions have become meaningless. Perhaps that's why I tune out the tanpura of family tales. Family woes don't appeal to me much; they don't move me like the rhythms and melodies of music.

Aranya laughed.

This is an oppositional enterprise. Why forget all that you've learnt all your life about family and clan, and confine yourself to reiterating truisms! Can you really reduce the meaning of family and clan to a few truisms? Not everything beyond family life is blissful.

Is it possible to do such a thing?

I don't know. It seems like differences have swallowed up that claim.

The lack must bother you!

If I say no, you'll begin to dig into psychological knots.

What's true is that I have begun to appreciate the calm of staying away from the tensions that underlie the superficial harmony of family life.

This seemed to make Ishan anxious.

Family relationships should not be interpreted in individual contexts alone.

Aranya laughed.

This could take up a whole Purana. Having dominance in joint families has to do with the individual's capacity to generate money. It's also about brothers and nephews observing their relatives narrowly, lying in wait so that they can capitalize on shifting moods and feelings.

Family bonds are deep, Aranya. There is much that is good and valuable, despite minor squabbles.

This upset Aranya.

The idea of the all-encompassing joint family has ceased to exist; it's a myth in today's day and age.

You're talking about a handful of wealthy people. The virtues of the joint family have become relevant again. Its roots have succoured our national culture.

I haven't known a joint family myself, Ishan. But what I have observed, from near and far, has not been pleasant. This I do know—it's those with lean accounts who pay the price for its ordered existence and social weight. The collective wealth of the family is managed like a business enterprise. Its inner power has waned. It provides no protective shade; rather, its tattered rags flutter in the wind. This may not ring true to you, Ishan, but I've seen it myself. And as I investigate it, at my own cost, I find that the golden truths bandied about in the name of its pure culture are a pack of lies.

Are you talking against it because you live alone?

No, Ishan. The working class girls I am talking about, they

speak up to me in thousands. And with them, the commonly acknowledged virtues and vices of the joint family surface to caution us. Believe me, this is not just oppositional, an attempt to be contradictory. It is an attempt to closely view what happens in society, what is happening in society.

I understand what you're saying up to a point, Aranya, but I still maintain that this needs more impartial investigation.

Aranya replied with sarcasm: Hearing you talk, one would think we were both heads of large families. With sons and daughters, grandsons and granddaughters. Their reference point for nurture. The graph of the business and professions of sons, the promotions of sons-in-law, their influence and achievement—that whole rigmarole happens to be absent in our case. You were talking about the house being silent, weren't you? That may be the reason for this.

I understand. Keeping your distance from the family must protect you from unhappiness.

Yes, it would be more correct to say that I'm never unhappy in my own company.

Ishan laughed sarcastically.

A marvel.

There's nothing marvelous about it. It's enough to understand, to know, that you're simply outside it, an event of which you're no part.

But the family one lives with is an open book. Mutual care is its solid evidence. No outsider can take away the intimacy of that experience.

There's plenty of experience of being left out of this charmed circle of intimacy.

How?

A child gets bad marks in exams; you're to blame, because you accosted the child as it was departing to take the exams. The son couldn't get admission to the desired school; your wishes came in the way. And if a boy or a girl didn't make the grade in some competition, the person who cast an evil eye on the child was surely the self-same *Trishanku*; belonging neither here nor there, left dangling in the middle, who asked after someone's job application, only to find out that it fell through. The fault lay once again with this person who belongs nowhere. Tell me how it's possible to survive such dear relatives and confine your interests to their horizon of expectation?

I have no near and dear ones, Aranya. That could be the reason why I find myself unable to agree with you. But I'm trying to see things from your perspective.

Being committed to such a family structure has to do with wealth and prosperity. If you participate in that, there'll be an abundance of affection and warmth. If not …

Are you speaking only from the daughter's point of view?

No, Ishan. These tales don't come from my own experience. I just know this that whether son or daughter, all members of a family have the right to alter their desires and disinclinations, sadness and joy, according to *their* wishes.

You're right about that, but don't forget, the family is a nest of security, the dense shade of mutual support. Family life is never monotonous.

Is there any point, Ishan, in glorifying the kind of protections which scrape away at your self-confidence?

Human relationships need the harmony that comes from growing and prospering in the confines of a family.

Aranya began to speak affectedly, as if she were play-acting: Yes, that's also an interesting state of affairs. Just last year, we went to the States. To be with the eldest. And before that, we were with the second daughter-in-law. She was expecting her second child. We go to our daughter when she calls us.

It's important to keep alive the need we have for each other. It's not a bad thing.

Ishan looked disaffected.

Does living alone give you the right to judge?

No, I've never lost faith in love or goodwill. That's why I'm not negative. But yes, I do have a critical perspective.

Imagine for a moment: One child is making us happy. Another is hell bent on making us unhappy. And a third is striding towards a golden future. A child's hair is being cropped for the first time, another is leaving to go abroad. But what if, as in our case, there is only one person to play all these parts, then apart from the noise of the television, what can we hope for. Can the silence behind its noise keep us entertained?

They both laughed.

We have no dearth of time. Should we now turn to the sons and daughters of families?

Only the family can discipline the haste and frenzy of the human mind. Countless unseen threads bind humans to society. Men and women develop their inner strength only by staying within the family fold.

Do men and women have different kinds of inner strength?

I see the sharp edge of your sarcasm begin to glitter again. It's interesting. Everything you say points outwards.

And yours inwards, and from inside towards the *atma*. Am I right?

You're not wrong.

My inner voice makes me relate to the flow of rivers. As soon as they leave their source, they gather speed. They don't stay fixed to one spot like mountains and highlands, with their heads held high.

Does the power of patriarchy make you nervous?

Yes and no, both. These two core stances of Nature no longer stand in hierarchical order. They face each other, so that they can fall into step with one another. The one no longer merely follows the other, as a follower trails a leader, they go as equals, in partnership.

Indian culture speaks of the *atma*, Aranya.

Aranya broke into laughter.

The *atman* of atma has become post-modern. Now it wants to buy pleasure and wealth along with Indian philosophy.

In what direction, Aranya, are you now dragging this discussion about the passage of the *atma*?

In the direction that modernity is taking us.

An unchanging depth lies beyond all the changes of life, Aranya. We humans will continue to exist on this Earth along with nature and science. Mountains, rivers, oceans will continue to coexist in consonance with each other.

Ishan, will patriarchy continue to uphold itself, and matriarchy continue to flow away? Will women ever have a right to the knowledge of *brahma*? Will she ever have the right to the knowledge of the *atman*? It is said, subjects as deep as philosophy are not meant for women.

No, the power to attain *brahma* comes from within—woman or man. Ishan knitted his brows.

Aranya looked at him with interest and said softly: It's almost time for your walk. How about we both have a glass of *mausami* juice?

Why not?

Four mausamis, a plate and knife were placed next to the juicer.

Ishan began to cut the mausamis cruelly, intently.

Aranya watched his hands for a while. Then in a playful

tone, she began to tease him: If I were to write this for the press from the perspective of a Mrs or Miss from the reservations quota, I would say that in this act of cutting, you demonstrate once more the prudishness of some ancient memory of your race.

What does that mean?

Aranya began to laugh.

Ishan watched her with disbelief.

Just this—squeeze out the juice and throw away the peel.

I speak not from my own perspective, but of those who ask for reservations quota.

six

Solitude. Dense desolation. Darkness.

What place is this? Water and sky, motionless, in one place. How? In their midst, a narrow, stony footpath.

Where am I?

Where do I stand?

There's a slight warmth in her body. Warm glow and cold tingle, both at the same time. The path from the sky reaches down to meet the narrow footpath! Take bold steps. Fly on the wings of wind. What colour is the wind? The colour of water is milky white, like glass.

Whatever it may be, scale its height.

Aranya's feet begin to touch the sky.

The phone by her bedside rang. She picked up the receiver.

Hello!

I want to speak to Aranya.

Aranya changed the timbre of her voice.

She's sleeping at the moment. Could you call in an hour?

In the haze of half sleep, she glanced at the clock. How did she get back to this world? I was looking at the shining sun in the skies, moon, moonshine, all at once.

There had also been something else.

A stole perhaps, or a shadow, a spectre, springing from the balcony. She felt the fear of it permeate her body. She cast aside the blanket. She splashed water on her eyes in the bathroom, brushed her hair, rinsed her mouth. Then she made tea and stood with a teacup in hand in the balcony.

She thought: I don't dream all that often. When I do, it's a sign of something or the other.

She strained her mind, searched the layers of her heart. Maybe it's a vision of some old fear. Something that the eyes haven't seen, something that merely appeared in front of them.

And why did her eyes need to view that scene? Was it the fear of the height from five storeys above the ground? Aranya leaned over the railing. Was it some desire—meek and mighty at once—to destroy herself?

No.

Below, there were rows and rows of parked cars, their speed exhausted. She saw herself with new eyes. An old life, this. Doubtlessly. But not yet stilled.

She opened the door and picked up the newspaper—and the bag of milk with the other hand. She noticed that the milk outside the flat opposite had spilled out of its bag, and the cat sitting in front of the lift was getting ready to lap it up.

She put an egg to boil in a pan on the stove, and pouring out the milk in a jar, she switched on the kettle.

Once again, tea working as a bellow for the body. It wakes up the body, no matter if it hurts or helps it in the final run.

The phone rang, exactly after an hour.

Am I speaking to Aranya?

Yes, speaking.

You don't know me. I'm a friend of Ishan's. We were neighbours in Curzon Road Hostel.

Yes.

I am inviting both of you to tea. I got your phone number from Ishan.

Please forgive me. I won't be able to come …

No, no, please don't refuse. I'll choose a day that suits you. I don't live all that far from you. My flat is just a five or ten minute drive from yours.

There was clarity in the voice.

Ishan was telling me, you won't be so busy the day after. I truly want to meet you.

Thanks. I'll come. At four-thirty, no?

Yes, I'll remind you at four-fifteen. Ishan will come with you.

Two days later, Ishan and Aranya set out for Damyanti's.

She used to be my neighbour. A happy-go-lucky creature. She was once very attractive, bubbly and energetic.

Ishan laughed, as if he saw her before him. Going up or coming down the stairs, if there was a whiff of perfume in the lift, we knew that Damyanti had either just left or just come back. Expensive perfume was her hallmark. Her husband was a decent soul. Lively, respectable and crazy about his wife. The children were left to the ayah to bring up. She turned to sadhu-mahatmas after his passing. A woman ascetic in Rishikesh is now her guru. She spends most of her time there.

Aranya was slightly put off. What will I do in that company, she thought. I'll get bored.

Ishan guessed what she was thinking.

You'll find her interesting. She's very modern. The way

she dresses, talks and lives. Women are usually jealous of her. Though she's changed now. We change one way or another as we age.

Do you find yourself to have changed much?

No.

And you, Aranya?

Me neither.

They seemed to be reassuring each other.

Damyanti welcomed them in a pearl grey suit. Ishan introduced the two women to each other.With her confident bearing, delicately applied make-up and her curly hair, she was the perfect image of a mature, well-to-do woman.

She circled Aranya with her arms and said: Come. She took them past the drawing room into her own room—Take a seat.

There was a sofa in one corner, a long table, a fridge and on the other side, a bed. Books and journals were arranged on a shelf. A glimpse of the past, of Delhi and Lahore, of the elegant decor of Curzon Road Hostel.

With a tray of water glasses in hand, Madho greeted Ishan.

Madho, you're well, aren't you? All well at home?

Yes, Sahib. You've come after a long time. Bahadur is still working for you, isn't he?

Yes, Madho. He takes care of dinner. He goes out to work in the morning.

There was honey and lemon in expensive glasses, ready for tea to be poured into them.

Ishan laughed.

You haven't forgotten.

How could I forget? I was thinking of you just yesterday.

Vaidya-ji says: Ginger juice, lemon and rock salt, the mixture is a universal remedy for all stomach problems. Tulsi and bel leaves as well. I don't eat meat and eggs any more, Ishan. I've become a vegetarian.

Amazing!

My very being has changed since I started living in the ashram. I have no desire to eat chicken, meat, fish. I couldn't have a meal without them before. There's been a great change in me. In the old days, I wouldn't let cotton clothes touch my body, Aranya. One day, just after the satsang, my guruji upbraided me. Now I've had sufiyana cotton suits made. Just listen to what my sons and daughters-in-law say. If I wear silk clothes, they say, this glitter and glamour no longer suits you at this age. But if I wear cotton, they don't like that either. You don't look like our mother any more. Now you tell me, what I should do?

Aranya flung her head back in distress: Wear whatever you like.

Damyanti laughed charmingly: You look like you rule over your heart and mind. Don't you feel depressed living alone?

No.

Sometimes at least …

No, never.

That can't be true. Come with me to my ashram. You'll experience deep peace. Do you have any interest in religion and spirituality?

No, I won't get much out of that. I keep busy otherwise.

No children, no family—what unfinished business do you have to take care of that you have no time?

Damyanti glanced at Ishan and laughed in a knowing way. Some work will always remain undone. We need to think what lies beyond.

Aranya's face altered in a way that Ishan thought it better to change the topic.

Is your younger son all right now, Damyanti?

Yes, much better than before. He can walk with help. His fiancée is with him these days. She helped my son a lot. She stayed on after the accident.

Tea was set on the table. Cake, biscuits and sprouts came with it. Damyanti poured the tea.

She said: Unit Trust has declared good dividends this time around. You must have also invested in them, Ishan?

Yes.

And you?

Aranya nodded vacantly. Such questions at the first meeting.

He took care of all my needs before he departed. In his last days, he would keep saying: I'll go first. What'll you do if you're left behind?

I used to laugh it off. Who has any control over life and death? If I go first, you'll marry some hussy.

He laughed at first; later, his eyes would fill with tears.

God knows how he had guessed he would go first.

We live the time allotted to us. We have no choice but to live through it. When it's time to go, we are alone. That is the law of creation.

Damyanti offered the plate: Please do try the papaya—it's sweet. Sometimes I add cream to it. It's wholesome. My guru takes a lot of interest in the food that is served at the ashram. I can't tell you how clean the kitchen is. The devotees make the pots shine.

Pure food makes for a pure existence.

Do come with me to the ashram. Why don't we go on some Saturday? We can come back by Monday or Tuesday.

I don't drive such long distances.

That's just an excuse. I have a driver, you know.

Aranya, you'll come, won't you?

No, no, that doesn't fit with my kind of schedule.

Damyanti watched her for a while with a faraway look in her eyes before she said slowly: This body with its eleven sensory doors, how will it get there. I've begun to worry about that now.

Aranya kept quiet, as if waiting for more entreaties.

When Ishan left them to go out to the balcony, Damyanti moved to sit next to her.

I've begun to feel afraid, Aranya. The fear of death, perhaps.

Put that fear outside you. Why should you be afraid of something that each of us is destined to go through?

It was as if Damyanti had her guru before her eyes.

My guru says, we are free in the performance of our karma but tied in experiencing its fruit.

Aranya cast a sharp look at her, then said softly: There's an ashram for the elderly nearby. Give some time to them.

What could I do there?

You could take part in their daily life. You could read out books and newspapers to them. You could write letters for them.

Damyanti's face lit up suddenly. Many thanks for that; I'll do that. I get so bored at home.

Why? You're not alone; your children live with you.

I would be less anxious if I lived alone, like you. My children stay with me. I run the kitchen in my house. I pay all the expenses. But I'm left alone in my room. They move my things about without my permission. I'm very upset, Aranya. When I went to the ashram some days ago, they threatened Madho: Tell us where Mamma keeps the key to the locker.

Why would I oppose them for anything? But they should also have some sense of duty. They don't bother whether I've eaten anything, whether I'm ill, whether I need medicine, tests, or a visit to the doctor—I do everything myself.

Bless Madho; I live on the strength I draw from him.

Aranya said nothing.

Say something, Aranya! My children's ways are testing my endurance. My son is asking for the papers of this flat. When I went to the doctor's the other day, my daughter-in-law had my divan moved to her room. She said, she liked it. And just listen to this, I don't have permission to leave this room. I can't have my guests sit in the drawing room.

That's wrong. Let's go sit there.

Damyanti's face became knotted with emotion. She whispered: I can't sit there, my guests can't sit there, even though I have bought the furniture and decorated the place. And I watch all this mutely, lifelessly.

Then she piped up when Ishan came back: We're getting more tea, let's go and sit there.

A well-appointed sitting room was lit up. Expensive furniture, heavy curtains, artwork from many regions, a Ganesha on a wooden pedestal, and spread beneath it all, a stunning Kashmiri carpet.

As mistress of the room, Damyanti began to chirp happily. She rang for Madho.

Yes, Sahib.

Another round of hot tea. Masala tea.

Yes, Sahib, I'll get it right away.

It was as if Damyanti had come home.

It's going well with Bahadur, no Ishan?

Yes, it's all right, I suppose. He makes dinner and keeps the house in order. I make lunch myself one way or another.

Sometimes, Aranya and I eat together. Our flats are not so far apart.

That's so good, Ishan. If only I lived there … Why don't we go on a picnic together sometime? Eat our lunch out under the sun?

I remember your picnic basket. Do you still have it?

It's still there. All my old things are. Only I am not in my old place. His departure has changed everything.

I'll make paneer for the picnic.

Damyanti laughed. Sindhi parathas with paneer. Madho is an expert at making them. There'll be just a touch of ghee. Aranya, will you fry the paneer?

Paneer can't be fried in water, but trust me, there'll be very little ghee.

The room echoed with their laughter. This burst of zest seemed to fill Damyanti with a new life. What will we have for dessert?

Nothing heavy. Plenty of fruit.

No, Ishan. I'll send for sandesh.

That will be perfect. Your old favourite.

The bell rang suddenly.

Madho opened the door. The second of the three sons entered with two guests.

He masked his anger as well as he could, seeing his mother in the drawing room with Ishan and Aranya.

Mamma, please take them to your room. We have something important to discuss.

We're drinking tea. As you can see, son …

How much more time will you take?

I've had to persuade them to stay on. They'll be here for a while.

Ishan and Aranya began talking to each other, as if they couldn't hear the dialogue.

Damayanti rang the bell for Madho with her son still standing in the doorway. Can you quickly fry some spinach pakoras? And don't forget to sprinkle clove and black pepper on them. There's some mint chutney in the fridge. Bring that too.

Yes, Sahib.

The son paced up and down the corridor even as the smell of ghee pervaded the air. There was anger in his footsteps. His seething hands hit out at the plate that Madho was carrying to the drawing room.

Damyanti rose from her seat when she heard the sound and moved towards the kitchen. What happened, Madho?

Nothing, Sahib. The plate slipped from my hands.

Damyanti ordered him in a calm voice: Pick this up afterwards. Fry some more quickly.

She looked at her son, then, and said sharply: Don't just stand there. Leave. I warn you. Don't you enter this house again. And understand this—I own this house, not you.

Aranya poured the tea into three cups and reached for the sugar and milk.

There was violence in the son's eyes.

Can't you hear me? Don't ever enter this house again.

From inside came the sound of the daughter-in-law crying.

Aranya and Ishan stood up to leave.

We're off, Damyanti. We'll fix a date for the picnic on the phone.

Aranya shook her hands, conveying silently to Damyanti: You have the right to do what you just did.

Damyanti's ageing face betrayed alarm. She pressed Aranya's hand and said: Stay with me tonight. My son is ruthless. He'll keep at it all night.

Calm down. You are responsible for yourself now that the children's father is no more. You also have the right to object. Believe me, he'll have to ask for your forgiveness.

Damyanti held on to Aranya's hand for a long time.

You have my phone number, don't you?

Damyanti nodded and gave Ishan a cold, limp hand, as if to ask for help of some kind.

Can anyone really help anyone else?

Three pairs of clammy hands. Is there any warmth left in them? Do they have the courage to confront today's children?

Love. Is that the only thing mothers have?

Do fathers, husbands, sons, still hold the strings of her person and her existence?

A month later, Madho called Ishan: Sahib, Memsahib has passed away. Her chautha will be held tomorrow.

What?

What happened, Madho?

What can I say on the phone, Sahib? You'll see when you come here.

seven

Aranya took out last year's clothes. The bright colours disturbed her. One should wear whites and creams. Is it accidental, the choice of this particular salwar suit?

No, she's taking it out because she wore it last year.

Why get tangled up with the past again?

You remember your date of birth, don't you?

Yes, how can one forget that?

And the significance of life?

Only a maze.

What is your primary accomplishment?

The evolution of mental and physical power.

And ambitions? Accomplishments?

It's not so easy to answer that.

Forget those now. Just recall the radiant days of childhood.

Aranya laughed. I am not a philosopher who can remain detached from good and evil.

Last year on this day, I lay stretched out in comfort. Rajen Kaul and Indu came by in the evening. They had brought a huge pineapple cake with them. They were both happy. Their happiness pervaded the evening.

She got ready, then looked at her face in the mirror. She laughed to herself. It still looks like my face.

What are you, Aranya? So self-absorbed.

Think about someone else for a change.

What is there to think?

These are all moot issues.

All this feeling and reflection must mean something.

Mere churning of reason and of imagination bubbling to the surface.

Why not look at the splendid diversity of the universe?

She looked at her reflection in the mirror again. There is no dust on the mirror, but that doesn't mean that you are as bright as you were once.

What do you call this season?

Vanprastha, old age.

Hail the advent of this precious season with another name.

It's a witness to time and experience.

You do know, don't you, that decades ago, two children playing on the lawn were separated forever. Shantanu, covered with blood in a road accident. His father left him at the place from which no one returns. Everyone has to reach there.

Aranya rebuked herself.

Forget the episode at Damyanti's today.

Those who'll have to bear the burden of our passing will take care of it.

There's a meeting at Ishan's place today.

She picked up the phone.

Wouldn't around five have been better, Ishan?

People like to go for a walk around that time, so I kept the meeting half an hour earlier.

I'd like to come ten minutes earlier, will that inconvenience you?

Not at all.

She put the container on Ishan's dining table.

Such a large cake. Why this, Aranya?

Today's a special day. Your birthday. Many happy returns.

And my good wishes on your birthday too, Aranya.

They shook hands.

We've crossed over to the other shore now, Aranya. Doesn't this seem childish to you?

Don't be upset, Ishan. I am only being myself.

Ishan couldn't help laughing.

Headstrong and persuasive.

Aranya said mischievously: There are two cakes, two containers. One for you and the other for me.

Why?

We were born on the same day, but we are two people. That's why.

That's not money well spent.

Aranya began to laugh.

It comes once a year, this day, and that too, only as long as we remain alive.

Ishan became serious.

I just have one suggestion to make, Aranya: Let's treat all days equally in this chapter of our lives.

Aranya spoke in the spirit of friendship: Unlike you, I don't regard myself as old. I am not embedded in a family where I see myself as an ageing mother or grandmother. The intimacy with myself gives me a sense of constancy, Ishan.

Ishan remained silent, as if finding her words excessive.

Aranya began to tease him.

It's not just the winds of the Pir Panjal mountain range that make you youthful. You have no second generation here to thrust you aside as 'old'. Those who are parents tolerate every situation and continue to live silently; they don't feel free to say anything.

You're negating so many things. A family is a deeply woven unit. The perimeters of its warmth, affection and love are regulated. It's a discipline.

Aranya laughed.

We need reservations and protective measures, rather than talk of the power of virtuous families to bind people together.

Ishan spoke with cold earnestness: There's a lot of difference between the way you and I think about this.

Oh yes. The difference between waking and sleeping. Between your self-knowledge and my rest and relaxation. Perhaps that's the reason why I don't read your Krishnamurti.

Ishan put his arms around her and touched her head.

Rest as much as you want and work as hard as you do. We're not likely to get much out of this conversation.

Two ageing figures broke into laughter.

The doorbell rings.

Namaskar!

Namaskar! Do come in.

Sardar Bhagat Singh.

Neither trim and slim, nor fat. High. Tall.

An unusual person, judging by his body and frame.

In his long steps, a glimpse of the miles he must have

traversed in his long life. He takes a bite every two or three hours and then wanders up and down to digest it. He says: The only secret to my digestive power—I eat a radish-paratha every day.

Sardar Sahib spends the second part of the week with his elder son and the first part with his younger son. He has educated his family, seen to their successful careers, and devoted himself now to getting his own world straightened out. To give shape to the experience gathered, he now counsels schools and other societies, writes articles on the health of senior citizens, and is getting ready to launch a journal for them.

Mr and Mrs Sundaram. A couple made for each other. The wife is an expert in classical music. Thrice a week, she gives lessons to children.

Did you call Mrs Vikramraj? She must feel lonely after her son and daughter-in-law set up their own home. She'll find that it is not so bad after all, this living alone. You don't lose touch with yourself if you're alone. You come nearer yourself.

Mrs Bhattacharya said: It's clear that the world of children is different from ours now. It's important to come to terms with the fact. Though it's true that the house loses all sparkle with the grandchildren gone.

Prasad said: Times change. With that, parents and grandparents have to change, too. It's a question of before and after, what used to be and what is.

Enter Rangachari with spouse. Supporting each other with each other's help. Close to each other.

Aranya watched them with curiosity. These people don't look like objects of pity.

They began to talk about books. About newspaper editors. About procuring new titles for the library.

A good part of the apartment complex rings with the

sounds of assorted regions. A pleasurable mix of Gujarati and Bengali.

Ila and Alok Desai. Deeply absorbed in and occupied with their own routines. The pressures of the day eases with walks and yoga in the morning.

Dwivedi-ji, who studied in Benares, arrived.

He is blessed with worldly comfort by the grace of his Bengali guru, and endowed with all the facilities, which any householder would wish for in life. Few people are destined to receive as much as he. Medical expenses are the responsibility of his sons. Like the other affluent few, the services of an expensive nursing home are available for all his minor and major ailments. Large and small body parts can be freed of ailments. The unlit corners of the day can be illuminated. Dwivedi-ji's discernment helps keep afloat spiritual and philosophical contemplation. His guru attained immortality, but he still hovers protectively over his student.

The door opened again and in came Mrs and Mr Ray. All their friends and neighbours wait for their Christmas and New Year parties. Brandy and nut-filled cake.

Enter Mrs and Mr Rajendra Prasad.

Bhagat Singh was saying: It's important for us to get to know the nature of our bodies, to recognize big and small ailments and to keep our blood circulation in order.

Sardar Sahib put forward his plan requesting support for his journal. The journal is ready for publication. As soon as we have a registration number, a title and a publisher, we would like to profit from your experience.

Bahadur set out the tea. Pieces of cake, savouries and sandesh. Why such a spread?

Aranya was shocked to see the cake. Bahadur had already cut it.

Ishan announced to everyone: It's Aranya's birthday today.

Aranya laughed and said: It's yours too, Ishan.

Congratulations to both of you.

Thanks.

Desai said: Interesting. Two neighbours with the same birthday.

Does the birth year also match?

Ishan and Aranya continued to laugh.

We're going to keep that a secret.

But why?

Bahadur was standing at the kitchen door, looking attentively. A devious smile reached the corner of his eyes.

Who knows why he was looking so strange.

Just then Sahni arrived.

Please excuse me. It took me longer than I thought to return from the slums on the Yamuna. We had to distribute slates and pencils to children there. They were so happy; you should have seen their faces. If all of you help, we could buy discounted blankets for them. If each of you donates one, then ...

Buy them from Khadi Bhandar; they'll be warm.

Ishan went inside.

He gave Sahni an envelope when he returned.

Your contribution is also there, Aranya. You can give it to me later.

Thanks.

Bahadur looked alert. Something like a shadow crossed his eyes and then disappeared.

Sahni looked at the list in his hands and said: And if we could get magazines from every house, we could have them picked up on Sunday.

How would it be if we dropped them off at our library?

The conversation continued over a second round of tea.

Aranya stayed on after the meeting, and asked for a another cup of tea.

Bahadur cleared the table quickly. A tray of tea arrived.

Aranya said: Please bring the cake tray as well.

No answer. The tap kept running and Bahadur remained silent.

Aranya looked at the table.

Still no cake.

She got up and went to the kitchen. The tray had been washed and the rest of the dishes were being rinsed in the basin.

She asked slowly: Where have you put the cake?

Oh that, I've thrown it away.

Bahadur pointed to the garbage can.

Why?

It's no good. Don't give it to Sahib to eat. Bahadur began to mumble: A demon sits in that corner. Demon. It's night. The sun will destroy it. I'll make an offering of rancid butter, tikki, bottle, meat and sweet bread to it on new moon night. Yes, my Narsingh devta won't let it be eaten.

Bahadur's eyes turned a fierce, murky red. A clamour of unknown voices emitting the sound of clashing sickles spread through the room.

Enough! Ishan handed his empty glass to Bahadur and said in a strict voice: Bahadur, get back into the kitchen.

Aranya watched the two of them. Then, as if cutting her words with a dagger, she said: A whole cake and the remainder of the cut cake were dumped into the trashcan.

Ishan hesitated for a bit, as if lost for words. Then he said softly: I am sorry, Aranya. This should not have happened.

He's possessed by a devata sometimes—an ailment hill-folks have. You must know about shamans. That's what it is.

I know nothing. All I know is that he's thrown my birthday cake in the garbage bin.

Aranya, try and understand what I'm saying. He doesn't know what he's doing when Narsingh devata descends on him.

You may believe in such things. Narsingh and Neech Singh—it's your problem, not mine.

Bahadur is not in his senses. Call it mental illness if you like.

Illness or artifice, I really don't want to know. But this I can tell you, I think it's wrong to believe and support such darkness and superstition.

I am leaving. Aranya went out of the door.

Birthday!

Cake!

More!

Hill shamans.

What a song! She opened the door to her flat and went into the kitchen. Switching the kettle on, she peeped into the garbage bin. She found her birthday lying there. What a wasted evening! A crazed Bahadur with rolling eyes, looking beyond Aranya's birthday—that blood-thirsty posture.

Aranya.

It was Ishan on the phone.

I want to come over for a while. May I?

No, Ishan, I'm feeling upset. I won't be able to talk to you. We'll meet some other time.

I'm coming.

The bell rang.

Aranya opened the door. She motioned to him to sit down.

I'm sorry, Aranya. This shouldn't have happened.

I have come to ask your forgiveness.

There's no need. Why should you ask for forgiveness? The one who should be asking for it is the one who was crazy enough to do this.

He's besides himself, Aranya, when the devata takes possession of him.

I know it now that I've seen it. His hand wanders involuntarily to the garbage bin.

Ishan spoke courteously: He's been with me since childhood. He has a weak brain.

The last time he was ill, he had to have a brain-surgery. When he could move about again, he said: Narsingh is my devata. I can see him. He has saved me.

Aranya flew into a rage.

Please don't tell me all this. I don't see sparks of light in superstitions, nor the seven primordial flames, which light up in the name of the gods of darkness.

Listen to what I'm saying, Aranya.

No, Ishan, did they insert a disc about devatas in his brain when they operated on him? It must have been the work of the surgeon, no?

What's happened has happened, Aranya. We can't reverse the situation. Ghosts and spirits, magic and spells, strike the uneducated, terrorize them.

Please leave me alone, Ishan. You won't understand why I am feeling agitated.

Ishan touched her hand: I know, Aranya. Why can't we forget the whole affair?

You're turning this into something trivial.

No, Aranya. Bahadur is almost illiterate.

Maybe. You're dumping the politics of having to discriminate between right or wrong on me. What makes you do that?

I beg to be excused. Let's go over to my place. Dinner's ready there.

No, Ishan. I'm not going to your place. I'll drink some milk before going to bed.

Silence reigned for a while.

Aranya asked: Is this the first time this has happened?

No, it happened last winter too. The neighbours across from me had gone to pay obeisance to the goddess. They sent *prasad* over when they got back. The bowl was lying on the dining table. When Bahadur came to put the fruit back after dinner, his eyes fell on the bowl. He kept looking at it and then his eyes turned red.

When I asked him to leave, the strange sound of a sickle came from his throat. Like a clatter. I couldn't understand what he was saying. His gaze was fixed on the bowl. Suddenly he began to tremble and screamed: Narsingh devata says this is polluted. Don't touch it! A gurgling sound came his throat, like sound caught in a cave. He looked fearsome.

I said firmly: Go inside!

The tap is still running. Go turn it off.

For a long time, I heard him grumbling in the kitchen. Gradually, he calmed down.

Ever since his operation, he says that Narsingh has saved him. His family thinks Narsingh takes possession of him.

You believe that?

I can't really say, Aranya. He came to me as a child. Now he has children of his own. People from the hills talk of shamans. I don't know whether it's superstition or a sign of fear, linked to some primordial instinct.

Ishan continued to muse for a while with his gaze resting on Aranya. Then he entreated her: We could go out somewhere and eat if you'd like that.

Aranya collected her thoughts, and then, as if some easy, spontaneous moment leapt into focus, she said enthusiastically: Let's go. I'll get my coat.

eight

Every evening a flock of the elderly comes to this small garden, first to walk and then to chat. Thanks to the Delhi Development Authority. People are grateful for the carpet of green grass in this tiny garden, for the beds of flowers, and the creepers. But for this pleasant little patch, they would find themselves gazing at a concrete jungle. Here, at least, a fresh wind blows. Tiny flowers adorn the garden like embroidery. Their presence is delightful. There is pleasure because there is air, there's sunshine, there's water. There's green on the earth and breath throbbing in this body.

We're old, no doubt, but we're not devoid of zest. We step out of the house, we buy all kinds of vegetables and fruit and return to the lap of our families, which we reared with our toil.

To have been relieved of work and toil and to enjoy domesticity ... This is the pleasure of being alive. The pleasure of being with the family is great, in spite of occasional rudeness, disobedience and indifference glimpsed in the eyes of sons and daughters-in-law. There is peace in the heart because everyone is together. Whether the shares go up or fall. That worry has its own upside and downside.

How refreshing, how valuable this span of time. Sitting on a bench and chatting, it doesn't feel like the sum total of one's labour and one's earnings has slipped out of one's grasp. That bundle is still attached to one's person. Quite another matter, that within the family, our rights have shrunk, and 'yes' and 'no' are now used with caution. In old age, freedom of choice becomes half or even a quarter of what it once was. One has to respect the wishes of sons and daughters-in-law. They should live the way they want to. Why should we go on issuing edicts?

Ignoring what we've said, not meeting our eyes, reminding us of our faults and errors— all this is part of family life … But in our last years, how good it is to hear our grandchildren say Dadu, Dadda, Dadaji.

nine

Finished with health, medicine, doctors, diets, yoga, the assembly of senior citizens turns to other topics. Pension, provident funds, price-rise ... Aranya rises from the bench nearby and begins to pace up and down another corner of the garden. A gentleman—only his back can be seen—is saying loudly: Times have changed. Living has become so costly that we can only wait for things to take another turn so that we can also live like those who call themselves ours.

Between her and the gentleman, there is a crowd of solitaries and twosomes, intent on their own needs and self-absorbed but also endowed with the ability to allow the needy to come by some things. Sometimes they cast a look that says, 'You've lived long enough. Vacate this seat now, make place for new people.'

The senior citizens keep an eye on each other. Who is waiting to go, who sees the signs in his chart and is upset and put out. And who is thinking about changing his will.

Someone gives the bungalow to one and the flat to the other. Someone takes away rights from the daughter and fills the fist of the son. Someone decides to ditch his love interest and take a new vow to remain faithful to his wife, thus sealing a deal in favour of his family before he's gone.

The old order still prevails under the guise of the new. Discriminating between son and daughter; killing the girl child in its womb and looking for ways to preserve the son. The unspoken conflict between son and daughter still rules the roost. The altercations between brothers and sisters still go on. There are new laws, but who puts them into practice? Only the parents can do so.

And those who opt out of the system apply these rules neither to themselves nor to the others.

We'll live as long as we live.

The narrative and logic of those who break away from the family is quite another matter. If you stand at a distance from the family, the myths of it glare at you from the other side of the fence. The family still is an institution of inter-relationships; it thrives on new and old histories.

How can the individual be absorbed into that? The individual will ripen in a laboratory outside the family, which he'll have to configure with his own strength.

Is that an illusion or a belief?

Gradually, the changes of yesteryear will merge with the new, and the new will also begin to age. The truths of consumerism will increase, and belief in relationships shall decrease.

ten

The gate was shut.

The windows were shut.

The garage was shut.

They opened the gate. That made a noise which triggered a harsh, apprehensive, frightened call from somewhere.

Who's that?

Who are you?

Khuku, look outside!

Ishan and Aranya walked to the porch.

The curtain in the bedroom window stirred, and through the grill peeped an old, pale face. Kamini.

Ishan went and stood at the window.

How are you, Kamini? It's been ages since we met.

The haggard woman behind the grill continued to stare.

She called out to Khuku when she recognized Ishan.

When no reply came, she said to Ishan, Go behind the garage and call Khuku. She has the key. She'll come and open the door from outside. It's locked.

Khuku. Open Memsahib's door.

Khuku opened the door with the key dangling from the end of her sari. She asked them to be seated in the drawing room.

She stopped Kamini, who was coming to join them, at the door: Wait, Memsahib, change your sari first. I'll take one out.

No, I haven't bathed yet. I'll change later.

This one is so crumpled, Memsahib.

Aranya and Ishan sat in the drawing room. Paintings hung from the walls. Memories from home and abroad.

Kamini who had studied in Benares and Allahabad had been posted in London once. She had been known for her beauty and quick wit.

She entered the room looking old and bereft. Khuku dusted the armchair. Kamini's taste from many years ago shimmered through the thin layer of dust that rose from it.

Khuku, don't you dust this room everyday?

Khuku's smile was covered by her silence.

Do sit down, Memsahib, everything is all right now.

Kamini sat down and continued to look around, as if she was in a neighbour's house, not her own.

Ishan asked: You're much better now, aren't you?

Kamini looked at Khuku standing next to her, as if waiting for a sign from her.

Khuku said: Things are much better now, aren't they, Memsahib?

Kamini nodded her head: Yes.

Then as if suddenly irritated, she said: You forgot to give me my medicine this morning.

No, Memsahib, you have forgotten. I gave it to you.

If I am saying I haven't taken it, who could you have given it to? Go get it now.

At that, Khuku cast a glance at Ishan and Aranya, and left the room with a smirk on her lips.

Kamini said: Ishan, listen to me. What happens if my signature isn't the same as the one at the bank?

Ishan looked this. Where was the alert, vigilant Kamini of old?

Aranya saw that Kamini's hand under the pallu of her sari had a slight tremor.

It would be best to meet the bank manager. The bank accountant can also certify that it's your signature. Our signatures do change from time to time.

Kamini noticed that Khuku was listening intently, and she flared up: Why do you stand around listening to us? Go do your work.

Memsahib, I'm the one who gets the money from the bank. It's important for me to know about this, no, Sahib?

Yes.

Khuku said impertinently: Memsahib has also lost the duplicate key of the locker.

Ishan and Aranya looked at each other in alarm. So the key to the locker was being searched for.

Kamini remained lost for some times. Then she said angrily: Go and make some tea.

The wan sunshine in the room that opened to the north began to fade.

Aranya looked outside. The withering green of the creeper on the window was a sign that the season was changing.

To fall silently like leaves, isn't that our fate too?

She took a deep breath, heaved a sigh and looked at Kamini.

The room was windless.

She rose and opened the long glass door, and a gust of wind blew in.

Kamini's eyes were drooping with sleep.

Ishan rose.

As he put a cushion behind her head to support it, Kamini woke up with a start: Who? What are you doing here?

I've put a cushion there so that you can rest your head, Kamini.

She gazed for a long time at Ishan and then said, turning to Aranya: Ishan. You've forgotten Lakshmi.

Ishan touched her lightly on the shoulder, laughed and said: Kamini, you're still siding with your friend.

Kamini laughed.

I know you well. You've fought with yourself, not with others. You love yourself alone. Am I wrong, Aranya?

Aranya smiled. At last something in this room had changed. A breath of fresh air had entered the old, desolate, expensive room. They heard the clatter of china from somewhere at the back.

Kamini started in alarm and began to scream:

Why did you open the door, Khuku? You want me to get bronchitis again? Is there any dearth of ill health around here?

Aranya stood up and quickly closed the door.

Kamini said softly: Thank you. This girl is such a dolt; she wants me to remain stuck in bed with one illness or another so that she can have free rein.

Aranya cast a stealthy glance at Ishan.

Khuku placed the tea tray on the table.

She put the medicine before Kamini: Please take this.

Kamini turned her gaze to the tray.

Have you brought nothing to eat with the tea?

There are some biscuits, should I get them?

Yes, there must also be some sweets in the fridge.

Khuku began to giggle. Baap re baap! How could three-month-old sweets still be there, Memsahib? They were eaten up ages ago.

How?

They were just turning stale, lying there. I distributed them amongst kids.

A cold anger clouded Kamini's eyes. As if she was thinking, this Bengali woman is now the mistress of the house, not I.

Go get some barfis or rasgullas from the market.

Ishan broke in: We ate something at home; we're completely full.

Aranya's soles began to itch the moment the tea was poured. As if the hoarseness in her throat brought on a lack of oxygen in her lungs.

She glanced at the floor as she was putting the teapot back on the tray. The bright Kashmiri carpet looked lifeless, as if it too had ceased to pay heed to itself. It must have adorned the floor when this house was first built. Pictures would have hung on these walls.

Bhaiya and Bhabhi are calling me to the farmhouse, Ishan.

Ishan said enthusiastically: You must surely go, Kamini. You'll recover quickly in the fresh air, sunshine and green over there.

Kamini listened attentively to him. Then she laughed as if in some kind of daze.

Kamini, you'll truly like it there.

Her face clouded. Bhaiya and Bhabhi are not calling me to their house, but to the farmhouse. The field is clear there. I could be strangled by anyone at all.

No, no, Kamini. It's not good to be so suspicious about everyone. They're your only close relatives. You've always looked after them; why wouldn't they care for you?

Aranya and Ishan both noticed that Khuku was standing close to the wall near the door.

Ishan called out to her: Khuku, go get a fresh kettle of water.

Kamini burst out in a helpless rage as she saw Khuku carry the tray off.

You were standing right here, weren't you? I knew you would be standing right behind the door. Ishan, those people have spoiled her. She gets money for the information she passes on to them.

If you go on talking like this, Memsahib, I'm going to quit working for you. Please settle my account.

Go get tea first!

There was a briskness in Khuku's steps as she left the room.

Aranya suggested: How would it be if you took in tenants in the annex upstairs? They would keep an eye on her.

Kamini said nothing. Then she beckoned to Ishan to come closer to her.

The broker has told me that my brother has sold this house. They've already taken the deposit. Khuku didn't tell me, but the builder has twice seen the house from all sides and he's been inside too. I was sleeping at the time.

Aranya and Ishan were filled with doubt and disbelief.

They were thinking: Is her mind unsound after all? Perhaps there is lack of blood circulation? Who knows what she's seeing or thinking? Her memory isn't helping her either. How can poor Khuku be expected to help her in this state? She's just a servant after all.

Kamini was saying: When I looked for them one night, I found the house papers missing from my file. When Khuku locked the door and went out the next night, I opened the cupboard again. I hunted through all the shelves. When I opened the file again, instead of the original, photocopies of the papers had been placed there … I don't have the originals any more.

The hair on the back of Aranya's neck stood on end. She stood up.

Ishan, I have to go the market. I'll be back in half an hour.

Then she turned to Kamini and asked: Tell me if you need anything.

Khuku was called again.

Go get the prescription from my table. You'll also find a list there. And bring some money as well.

All this was entrusted to Aranya and she left the house.

How suffocating. It was impossible to breathe inside!

Ishan asked Khuku: You keep the keys to Memsahib's cupboard, don't you?

Sometimes they're with Memsahib, at other times with me. She can't remember things. She forgets after keeping them somewhere, and then I'm showered with abuse. What am I supposed to do, Sahib? I could quit this job, but she's in such a state—I feel sorry for her.

Treat her like your mother. It's fallen to your lot to look after her; you'll be rewarded if you serve her well. God will be pleased with you.

Kamini was calling out: Lock the cupboard and give me the keys.

I'm bringing them, Memsahib.

Sahib, I live in the room above the garage. Ask Memsahib to have it transferred in my name.

Ishan was startled. How can that happen?

Nothing is going to remain hers, Sahib. Her brothers have already sold the house. If I had a paper in her handwriting, I could also make a couple of thousand.

When did her brothers come to meet her?

They never meet Memsahib. They come with the contractor or engineer three to four times in the week. But they stay outside.

And Memsahib, does she...

She sleeps most of the time. The doctor must be giving her sleeping pills. She's dead to the world when she's sleeping. She was awake one day, Sahib, when she saw her brother outside. She started yelling. There was so much shouting and cursing ... A lot of people gathered.

Has the doctor prescribed sleeping pills to her?

I don't know, Sahib. I buy from the chemist whatever's written.

Can you read the prescription? Do you know what medicines to give to her and when?

Khuku became defensive. Sahib, now you're getting suspicious too. I get the chemist to put marks on the medicine strips for me.

You have his telephone number, don't you? Just dial it. Let me speak to him.

Khuku stood there, sunk in deep thought.

Then she said softly: There are two sets of doctors, Sahib, not one. On Tuesdays, the brothers' doctor comes by. I do whatever he tells me to do.

And the other one?

He's Memsahib's old doctor. I can't understand what he says.

As Ishan turned to go inside, Khuku said: Her elder brother

has told me that she'll be moved to a nursing home in a couple of days. He's asking for Memsahib's keys, Sahib. How long can I keep them hidden from him?

Ishan peeped inside.

Kamini's eyes were shut and the cushion had slipped from under her head into a corner of the sofa. It occurred to him to touch her to make sure she was all right.

But then, in a nervous haste, he left the room.

Khuku shut the door to Kamini's room.

All right, Khuku, we're off. Look after Memsahib.

Yes, Sahib, but that paper about my room …

This is something only Memsahib's brother can do. Discuss it with him whenever he comes.

Aranya was almost running as she came back and handed the packet of medicine to Khuku.

As she handed over a second packet, she said: There's ice-cream and pineapple cake in this one. Give them to Memsahib for sure. She can easily eat them.

Yes.

Khuku's eyes began to gleam. Aranya handed her some money:

This ice-cream isn't for the kids. I've bought it hoping you'll give it to her.

Khuku nodded: Yes, Sahib.

They sped along in silence for ten kilometres.

There was little left to say to each other. It was as if a dead stillness plumbed the depths of their heart and mind. Are we also going to face this?

No.

A long, wide bridge joins the two shores—the two shores of age— and then, there's the end.

Ishan entered the gateway. He heaved a long sigh as he parked the car in the garage.

Their blocks of flats, their floors, the laundry drying on the walkway, everything was known and familiar. Just as they'd left it in the morning.

Thank god, nothing had changed here.

They proceeded to their respective blocks without exchanging a word.

Aranya entered her flat and went straight to the bathroom. She washed her hands and face, changed her clothes, pulled a brush though her hair and, who knows why, tied it in a tighter knot.

Let go, allow it to end, this business of ageing. Kamini must be younger than you … Can't you forget what you've just seen?

Oh!

The thought of Kamini, again and again. She reprimanded herself: Let this wash away. Forget her misery; she needs help. But can one person really help another? An old-age home … ? That is the only remedy, perhaps. Where are those people who used to care for others? Where are the families of yore?

The lush green flowerpots from the balcony opposite hers are peeping in. There's a bird hopping on the vine climbing over the window.

But what's this? Kamini's old face peers in from across the flowerpots. If only Kamini could also grow in the balcony of some house. Why, she could grow in her own balcony.

What a house that was.

There was sunshine and there wasn't.

There was breeze and there wasn't.

It was as if all the oxygen had been sealed in some cylinder and locked.

Kamini had worked hard in her professional life. There had been no dearth of money. She had earned her pension. Then why did this happen to her? Her body chained by illness and her soul in anguish, she'll reach the nursing home soon and the house will be lost. A new building will come up in its place. Lying there, Aranya thought: Kamini, why couldn't you anticipate your future? You studied astrology in Benares, didn't you?

She put on some music. The twang of sitar strings sent a shiver through her.

Are body and soul one?

No, the body is merely the sheath.

Such disregard for the body.

Aranya seemed to be looking at the next leg of her journey. What did she see?

That which no one wants to see.

An afternoon which made the heart tremble. Was it really necessary to have gone there?

When Kamini fell sick last year, Khuku had phoned him. Kamini had had a heart attack and was in a nursing home.

Brothers and nephews showed up but complained that she hadn't written a single post-dated cheque. She trusted no one and confided in no one.

Ishan had felt awkward.

In a week, Kamini was out of danger. When he went to

see her, Kamini asked Ishan: Will you be able to write two cheques for twenty-five thousand each? I'll have to pay the bill before I leave. I'll pay you back when I get home.

Ishan had written two cheques and she had returned the money. But when he went to see her one evening, her brother came and sat next to him.

Ishan bhai, she doubts everyone. No one has any sense of her accounts. And she's unpredictable. She likes the son of one sister one day, another on another day. She is entirely indifferent to the sons of her brothers. She used to share things with Lakshmi didi. Do you have any idea where she has made her investments?

Ishan said: Please forgive me. These are family matters, I know nothing. I came to the nursing home when Khuku phoned me.

The brother asked in a strange, unfriendly voice: What was the figure on the cheque that Kamini returned to you?

Two of twenty-five each.

The brother frowned angrily.

There's been no question of returning what I've spent on her.

Ishan stood up. I'll leave now.

Ishan had a long history with Kamini. She and his wife Lakshmi had been friends. They were colleagues and had taught together. After Lakshmi left, something very natural had developed between the two of them. And then for some reason, some lack of trust, awkwardness had crept in. What fate! The webs we weave … I've been fortunate. Why am I thinking about all this?

However patient she may be, this must irk Aranya.

She fled from the claustrophobia of Kamini's house to buy something from the bazaar. Quick empathy …

Aranya was watching Khuku with mocking eyes, but also the two of us. How could one tell what she was thinking?

Evening came. Ishan was in a quandary. Should he phone her or not? Who knows how she is feeling after coming back from that house.

He dialled her number.

Aranya, did you have anything for lunch?

Yes.

What?

Chapati and omlette. And there was some paneer left over from yesterday.

Then there was a long silence.

I can send over some cassettes if you like.

No thanks.

I'm sorry I asked you to come with me. There was no need to trouble you.

Aranya said softly: I don't know why I am feeling scared, but after seeing Kamini, I find myself questioning everything around me.

Aranya, do I hear right? Scared and you?

Ishan, say something to reassure me.

Aranya, we are free to act, only unfree to bear the fruit of our actions.

Ishan, not these aphorisms. You know, after returning from Kamini's, it feels like we, too, have stepped into a parallel universe.

What makes you think so? We're no strangers to this world.

Ishan, Kamini's silence was hurting you deeply. As if you were responsible for getting her into this fix.

Aranya, she was Lakshmi's friend, not mine.

Aranya began to laugh.

I'm not asking you about that. I am just stating what I saw in her.

The phone rang at dinnertime.

What if we ate together?

Ishan, I've cooked nothing till now.

Dinner's being made here. I'll bring it over. You'll just have to wait for fifteen minutes.

Thanks, Ishan.

Aranya rose.

She freshened up and took stock of the table.

She arranged the placemats, changed the napkins and brought out two plates.

Two plates on one table.

As long as it lasts …

Ishan will have made khichri, vegetables, with a dollop of butter on top!

She took out some fruit from the fridge and put them in a bowl. That cheered up the table.

Forget the afternoon at Kamini's. That's the only cure.

It's evening now.

Remember, each day is a blessing.

The doorbell rang.

Aranya's old feet began to dance.

Ishan!

eleven

Sometimes, one finds the right resolutions to old feuds, at other times, the wrong ones. Older people, left on their own, away from their families, have different problems and muddles. Enveloped in their own pathos, their existence is shaped by possibilities and hopes gone stale. Sometimes, they are at peace with the uncertainties of body and mind; and at other times, they fret over illness and anxieties—blood pressure moving high and low; pulse racing or crawling; abstaining from sugar and salt ... Doctors' prescriptions are made according to the social status of the patient. In case family funds are limited, medication comes from the Central Government Health Scheme. But if the sons are professionally employed, the responsibility of providing medical care is theirs. And if there is too much wealth and too many means, there's an excess of medical tests. Also, from the parallel universe of Yunani and Ayurvedic treatments, advice and dosages keep flowing.

This group of elderly comes out every evening to meet in this small garden outside their homes, away from the closed evenings of the younger generation, making it easier for sons and daughters-in-law. One's rights shrink with time. Pranams and namaskars is what they get in return for the blessings they shower. The warmth and oppression of living with the family, both come at once. The pre-conditions and predicaments of age.

Then there is the shortage of space. The children aren't entirely in the wrong. In flats with just two or three bedrooms, two generations have to somehow make do with each other.

There are discussions about sons and daughters. About those who live in America, England, Australia, Dubai, about how they need the maternal and paternal grandmothers to take care of their small children, about how they send air-tickets from abroad, and about the meeting of the young and old in unusual locations. They also talk about the senior citizens who have no family at all in the vicinity. They are few in number, they have fewer responsibilities.

There is a clear awareness of caste and class in this assemblage of disparate origins. Within a particular class, there are some people who follow and some who lead. Those who fall in between have their own preoccupations and daily routines. There's no one to oppose them in any way. They can live as they please, as long as they are alive.

This cluster of senior citizens keeps a silent watch on each other.

Who's skipping the daily walk.

Who's being seen ever so often at the doctor's.

Who is in deep thought at sunset.

Who's making mental changes in his last will.

Who is turning over the flat to the daughter.

Who is depriving another of it.

Who is ignoring intimate relationships for fear of embarrassing the family.

Who is sealing the claims of the family as his last obligation.

Who is donating how much to which charities.

There is a much larger number of solitaries than before. They have their own difficulties and privileges. Separated from families, they lead a disciplined life, in accordance to their financial constraints. Protecting themselves from the myriad family anxieties, saving the strength collected, drop by drop, for eventual illness, unexpected trouble, they remain engrossed in their own world, doing some good work for the very young and the very old from time to time.

The solitaries have their own lifestyle. They engage in self-construction and preservation.

Not for them, the noise and tumult, the highs and lows, the tensions of the family. Still, when from the shadows of the past, a memory is savoured of the father's feet, the mother's hands, brotherly or sisterly affection, there wells up a longing for the warmth of the mother, the love ripened in the discipline of the father.

twelve

In a flat nearby, in the last few days, the indecorous became decorous.

Prabhu Dayal, a widower, was alienated in his own house by his three sons. His miserly, secretive persona began to irk his sons. They began to track his routine. At all times, there was a key dangling from a thread round his neck, and a lock on his room whenever he left it. The sons and daughters-in-law were upset. Who knows what all dear father is hiding from us. Rumours were doing the rounds that he was involved in a big project and had been often seen in Meerut.

Prabhu Dayal was stunned one morning to see his sons waiting for him when he entered his room after his bath and recitation of Hanuman Chalisa.

He cast a silent glance at them, and taking the clothes from his bed, dressed himself. Maintaining his fatherly demeanour, he asked: How come so early this morning?

The eldest son stared into his father's old eyes with his new business-minded ones and said smoothly: Babuji, you'll need to withdraw money from your account. If we don't pay up today, we'll be locked out of both the factory and the shop.

Why did you let it come to this? Why didn't you tell me earlier?

All this later, Babuji. We tried till late last night, but we couldn't raise funds.

The fury on Prabhu Dayal's brow pierced right through his sons.

The youngest, his favourite, avoided meeting his father's gaze, which looked to him for assistance.

The second son spoke: There is no time to dilly-dally. You'll have to do the needful …

Me, what do I need to do? The work is yours, so you'll have to take care of this.

The eldest barked at the second one: Take hold of his key.

Before Prabhu Dayal could touch it, the second son had snapped the key dangling from the thread around his neck. What greater contempt could they have shown their father?

Open!

To save his dignity, Prabhu Dayal said: Here, give it to me. Why don't you ask Raghuvar, your father-in-law?

He's also your in-law, Babuji. He's the one who's told us what you're up to.

How dare you talk like this?

It's the truth, Babuji. You're tied to a house in Meerut. Who is that woman?

Shut your mouth!

That won't work, Babuji. We'll need to find marriage alliances for our own children soon.

Prabhu Dayal screamed: Enough of this jabber now!

The sons clambered down, having done with Babuji.

Prabhu Dayal shut the safe. He slid the key underneath his pillow and was about to lie down when the youngest son entered the room again and said: I forgot my watch here … I've taken this out from Barey Bhaiya's file. Just read it. I'll put it back on his table afterwards. I'll have it coming, otherwise.

Prabhu Dayal lifted the bottle of Califos from his bedside, took a dose and began to read the document. He kept turning it around and looking at it. On the letterhead was the address of a detective agency.

He caught his head in his hands. This ruse is Raghuvar Dayal's. Prabhu Dayal began to feel weak. It felt as if they had sucked all the blood out of him. His daughter-in-law peeped in a couple of times. There was contempt in her eyes, as if she were saying: A home outside the home. At this age? Another woman!

When Prabhu Dayal got up to go to the bathroom, he gazed at himself in the mirror. Do I look as old as the boys consider me to be? Good-for-nothing ungrateful wretches, engrossed in their own families and weekends. Don't I know them? I'm their father, after all.

A week later, Prabhu Dayal was sighted once more in Meerut. On high alert now, he looked around to see if he was being followed. He sauntered, as if out on some errand. He bought a sari and a box of sweets from Begum Bridge.

When he ate the light phulkis Kalavati had made for him that evening, he felt happiness wash over him. Not for a moment did he feel that she was another woman. How jealous the boys feel that she is there for me. What could the boys have done if I had married her.

He informed Lalaji that he would be leaving this rented house soon and get his own house by next month.

A thunderbolt has struck this business family.

Funerary white sheets have spread on red and black-bordered durries. Friends, relatives, acquaintances are all participating. Whispers rise from the white sheets. The world is full of enticements, and Lala Prabhu Dayal was ensnared in them.

After the death of his wife, Kalavati, the daughter of his maternal uncle, enlivened his life like a flowering vine. Attached to her were her brothers and nephews. Gossipmongers said that the factory in Meerut was destined for them. Many secrets will come to light when the police unravel this conspiracy.

Prabhu Dayal's car was halted on his way back from Dehradun, Saharanpur and Meerut. Forty-eight hours later, a report was registered with the police. Prabhu Dayal's car was found parked in the garage and the driver was on truck duty for the factory. In the last few months, Prabhu Dayal had become suspicious of his driver. He had begun to come and go by train or taxi.

The postmortem disclosed that he had been strangled to death. His corpse was found beneath a tamarind tree, a few kilometres from Hindon. The family plunged into mourning when they got the news. What had to be came to be. Golden biscuits and another woman!

With grief-stricken faces, the sons listened to Pandit-ji's discourse: Lalaji was so enterprising. Active to his last day. He fulfilled all his family obligations like a good householder. For his three sons, he set up three factories, then became engrossed in his grandchildren after the passing of his wife. But who can erase what fate has destined for one?

The family is making undisclosed donations in his hallowed memory.

Pandit-ji's discourse is on.

Release by death is also a re-release.

After all, it's also important to sift and trim the vast universe the Supreme Being keeps in rotation.

As a good karma yogi, Lalaji left for his heavenly abode

only after he had brought his estate in order and seen to his family's comfort and prosperity. It is with peaceful hearts that we offer him tribute, vowing to keep his good deeds alive in this world by continuing to uphold the dharma of mankind.

As per the instructions from his family, Pandit-ji is winding up his discourse, avoiding all topics which can cast suspicion on anyone:

Ladies and gentlemen, please to remember that every now and then, even the gods are filled with desire and hope as they pray—O Lord, in your supreme grace, make it possible for us, on whatever occasion you find appropriate, to be born in the world of mortals. The gods in their heavenly abode have become rather tedious for us now. You have caused all treasure to flow to the mortal world. Are you now relegating us to the category of the scheduled caste? Spare us that fate, Lord. Will we have to fast outside your parliament? Lord, you may well be trying to keep these truths and facts well hidden, but meanwhile, please send us instantly into the world of mortals.

In this hour of need, we may well be able to contribute our bit to the welfare of mankind.

thirteen

Hello, Aranya!

Hello, Ishan!

How was your trip?

I had a comfortable journey. The train was a bit late, but I reached all right.

How was it there?

Good. People were pleased.

Could you find some time tomorrow? Around four?

Why not?

I am going to surprise you.

Aranya laughed.

How am I supposed to wait till tomorrow?

I'll come by this evening for a bit, if it's fine by you.

Ishan looked happy when he came over.

I want to show you something.

Ishan took two photos out of an envelope.

These are my daughters. This is Aparajita. This one is Shrishta.

Wow!

Aren't you surprised ?

No, Ishan.

Won't you ask where these daughters were until today?

I know it's easy to come by daughters, if they have not been destroyed in the womb.

Look at the letter they have sent me.

Dear and respected Pita-ji,

Greetings from both of us. Children from our school are coming to Delhi for Republic Day. Didi has said that we'll be able to meet you. We received the photo you sent. We were very happy to get it. We look at it every day when we're done with our homework. My sister and I want to buy shoes in Delhi. Didi says you'll help us buy shoes we like, and a chocolate each.

With love,
Aparajita and Shrista

It feels good to think that these girls are mine. These projects that integrate children into families work very well. You can contribute a bit to the education of these children.

Ishan, I had also wanted to be part of some such project, but gave up the idea when I thought of the headache involved in bringing up children. There is a programme where you can call the children over to your house for their vacations. It's enough if they can stay at your place just for the summer break.

Can you suggest things I could get for the children? I have to meet them tomorrow.

I am to be their father for the next two years. You may want to take this as a suggestion, Aranya. You could also become the guardian of daughters from the orphanage for the next three to five years. All you have to do is send a cheque to the institution.

Do you expect to see any change in me if I do that?

Ishan grinned. Not one bit. That's not what I expect. It's just one's social duty.

I'll think about it tonight and let you know.

Aranya felt that Ishan had left the children there, in her house, when he took his leave of her.

She phoned him. We'll have to give the girls something to eat.

How about making semolina laddus for them?

Could you make them?

Why not?

Aranya laid out semolina, ghee, sugar, almonds, raisins, browned them on low heat and made laddus.

Aparajita was eight years old and Shrista six.

Frocks, socks and shoes. Ribbons. Things were being readied for the children.

She cut out pictures from calendars, magazines and pasted them on old invitation cards. Then she took out a ream of coloured paper and put them in two envelopes.

Instantly, the house assumed a different feeling.

She searched out old stamps and coins from many countries, and put them in two little boxes.

Charming amusements, these. Where on earth did these two girls come from? They had only just set foot in Delhi and already filled up the house. As if childhood was keeping the house astir.

Ribbons of varied hues, shoes, socks, books, pencils, erasers—their arrival kept not only two houses abuzz but also two hearts.

Let's see how we, and the two daughters, welcome the

morrow. Ishan had left behind some books and some papers for Aranya.

She took them off the table to store somewhere.

There was a time when one found interesting papers in books. Romantic, intoxicating days … Where did they go?

She laughed. They must be crouching in some nook.

I am getting excited. Youthful days. Fresh seasons. Where had they flown?

Should I go and look at myself in that mirror? No, no …

That's enough for today.

She unfolded a sheet of paper.

Shunyata's letter unfolded in her hands.

She was on alert instantly.

fourteen

One way or the other, we recognize the signs of our times.

'Can you hear the clamour of the seas? The deep bellowing of the wind? The roaring silence of Shunya, emptiness, that is what they are. The seas and the firmament are the two vistas of life. Life and light. The life-force of the firmament and the radiance of light. The limitless reach of water, wave for wave, playing on Earth. And yet, go closer to it and the innermost reach fills up with emptiness.

Is disappearing into the limitless, into Shunyata, the destiny of mankind?

'Just as the river becomes still and pure when it reaches the sea, so the water becomes celestial in the arc of clouds.

'The golden dawn of the Himalayas, when will I be able to see it? Walking along the shore of the sea, when will I near the peaks of the Himalayas?'

Shunyata's lines were pulling Aranya to those icy peaks where the boundless treasures of the Himalayas lie. As if a soft breeze were blowing through her mind and body. As if her eyes could see the dazzling white peaks.

Aranya had just come back from shopping when the washerman brought back the laundry. Seeing the heavy curtains washed clean made her feel that some burden had been lightened. The curtains' cotton lining saved them from dust and grime, but made them so heavy that it was difficult to hang them up on one's own. Made of small brainwaves and failures, this, our middle-class. The curtains have changed over the last twenty years courtesy of careful washing or dry cleaning. The weave that has frayed in places has been darned; it will hide in the folds of the curtains.

She asked Ramkhelavan Dhobi: Bhaiyya-ji, I won't be able to hang up the curtains myself. It'll take you some time to hang them, but I'll take care of that.

Ramkhelavan was reassured.

Ramkhelavan fetched a ladder from the balcony and began attaching the hooks to the curtains.

The kids are going to school, aren't they?

Yes, Sahib, I have a B.Sc. myself. How could I let the children go without education? We are Kabirpanthis, Sahib. We understand the importance of education. Though I still follow my ancestral profession, my children won't be doing this.

How is the little daughter doing?

She is very quick, Sahib. She sits with her brothers and says: I also want to read this.

That's a good thing.

The eldest son is in class ten, Sahib. Goodness, what kind of boys he hangs out with nowadays; he says the strangest things. He's good at his studies. He says he wants to be an engineer.

In that case, you should have no complaints.

He was asking me the other day: Papa, why did Dashrath Maharaj banish Ram to the forests?

I explained to him: Maharaj Dashrath had given his word to Rani Kaikeyi, son. When Rani Kaikeyi asked him to fulfill his promise, Maharaj Dashrath could not refuse. He was a Kshatriya after all. It was in this context that Tulsidas-ji wrote the lines—This has always been the way of the Raghu clan; keeping your word even if it costs your life.

To which my son said: What are you saying, Papa. Did Ram-ji get no education?

He got it straight from a guru.

Why couldn't he tell Kaikeyi and Dashrath that what they were doing was not right?

I didn't like my son saying this, Sahib. So I scolded him: What nonsense are you talking.

What I'm saying is right, Papa. Ramchandra-ji was the eldest prince of Ayodhya. He had already married Sita maiyya. His father banished him to the forest. If Mummy were to ask you to do something so lame, would you agree to do it? Were there no ministers in Maharaj Dashrath's court to advise him against this? Should you banish someone destined to accede to the throne to the forest, just because of something a stepmother said?

Look here, Munna, focus your attention on your studies. I don't like the way you argue.

Ramchandra-ji was older than his brothers, Papa. Why didn't Maharaj keep him back? He could have explained things to Rani Kaikeyi. Did they have no people and panchayat in those days? They must have had some laws and customs in the royal family, Papa … ?

Keep your mouth shut, Munna. You're finding fault with

someone who is known as Purushottam Ram, the most superior of all men.

I'm speaking of Dashrath Maharaj, Papa.

Sahib, at that I lost my temper. I shouted at him. Shut your mouth. I won't hear another word.

Do you know what he said to that?

He said: It's likely that Dashrath Maharaj did not want to hear anyone out, just like you. He must have colluded with Rani Kaikeyi. That's why he fell so sick.

I tell you, Sahib, I was ready to beat that boy. It was difficult to hold myself back. I thought to myself, he must be repeating what he hears bhangi-chamars say. All of this is the roguery of the low-castes, Sahib.

I tried to explain to him: Son, why would you want to be called a born and bred dhobi by talking like this? It isn't as if our people haven't already caused pain to Sita Maiyya before this. It was we washermen who slandered her and had her sent through the ordeal of agnipariksha. Aranya was perplexed.

Ramkhelaven said: It isn't as if the upper castes haven't spread their share of hate. They call themselves cultured and Dalits and the Scheduled Castes uncouth, uncultivated and inferior. As for reservations, sometimes it's the Manuvadis who get upset and sometimes the Dalits and poorer classes. It's the profession of politicians. Who knows how long they'll go on playing their politics just so that it goes on? Brahmin with Brahmin, Baniya with Baniya, Thakur with Thakur, Yadav with Yadav—how many communities are you going to set up under one Constitution, Sahib? Why doesn't Parliament enforce the Constitution strictly? The high castes abuse girls of the lower and backward castes and stroll around freely, stroking their mustaches. This is absolute injustice, Sahib. It's a crime. No act becomes good just because it gives pleasure to you and me. It's desirable only if it gives pleasure to many. Doesn't democracy mean participation of the majority? And the police? If they are high-born, they'll just stand and watch. They'll use the law to bury all evidence of crime. The daughters of the weak will continue to weep and beat their breasts.

The curtains had been hung up. If the light and wind coming in through the doors and windows are obstructed, let it be so; curtains protect us from dust and pollution.

The nation is our home.

May curtains continue to flutter in the wind.

May the poor and unlettered castes continue to be oppressed.

May daughters and daughters-in-law continue to be raped.

Nations are meant for classes, pure and virtuous.

That's what Ramkhelavan had been trying to say.

Aranya touched the cloth bag of lentils, turned it around, felt it with her hand and hung it above the sink again. It'll take a couple more days to sprout.

Grains and seeds can sprout, and continue to sprout, but not we ancients. The old and the ancient dry out slowly. Like us. We leap over decade after decade, wanting more and more from life. The greening seasons make fresh blood flow, even in old shells. They are absorbed into the body.

Astonishing all the same, the fragrance of fresh earth on the shutters of the mind.

Ignore it all, Aranya, forget it. Don't remember dates. Just go on living.

And why is that bad? Isn't there still that responsiveness which flutters into being when clothes brush against your body? It sparkles every now and then, and when it does so, dark valleys bask in the sun. The winds swing in its primeval song. And the body fills with unspoken, incomprehensible words. Is all of this an illusion? If that were so, why would the procedures of life and death, efforts to relieve oneself of illness, life insurance, be contrived?

Age doesn't allow itself to be deceived. It contains the essence of all that has been lived.

The municipal birth certificate has to be invalidated, the certificate of departure issued. But it is the others, not we, who have to be prepared to carry out these tasks.

The journey between these certificates slides on with help from memory and desire. Why be unresponsive if we encounter someone on the way?

She peered out from behind the glass on the balcony. The grey of concrete, and above it, the blue sky. The sky does not seem as distant as a while ago. Astonishing and marvellous, nonetheless. Each day is deep and pleasurable, just as each decade. Only that which is close to life and living is good.

How comfortable this house has been. But all that lies ahead is uncertain. I've been looking at barsatis, houses, rooms at the back, and airy flats without lifts. Two large rooms but a useless bath and toilet. If the house is all right, the stairs are dangerous. Open, airy house, but the neighbourhood unknown. A heroic saga, this search for a house.

The morning had been full of promises, but it faded and sank into evening.

Back after a long afternoon away from home, Aranya found that the next move was absolutely unclear. She had no clue where to set up a home after uprooting herself from here.

Just as she was about to finalize a deal after having seen a flat, the elderly man standing next to the agent had asked: Who'll be taking responsibility for you?

Responsibility for me? What do you mean?

Will you be living here alone or will someone else live with you?

I'll be staying alone, and I am in charge of myself.

What is the year of your birth?

Why do you ask?

Because we need to ask.

Why would we want to be involved in any trouble after your passing?

Aranya glared at him. Then she said, coldly: I don't want this flat. Give it to a tenant who doesn't plan to die.

The flat she had seen the other day was not bad. Only the woodwork awaited completion.

The agent asked for lease by the firm.

She agreed. Yes, I'll be able to give the lease.

Please let us know the name of your firm.

My publisher.

Are you a writer? Do you write books? If that's the case, how will you be able to pay your rent?

Aranya climbed down the steps without giving any answer.

The agent followed her: I'll persuade the owner of the flat. It's his daughter's flat. She lives in Canada. You'll need to give an advance of three months' rent, three months' security and three months' advance for water and electricity. Any changes in the house will be at your expense, but that will be deducted from your rent over time.

Thank you so much, Dalal Sahib, please look for another tenant. I don't want your flat.

She called Vinita when she came back home. Vini, your transfer isn't about to happen, is it?

At least not for another year. Why, what's up?

May I keep my stuff at your place and stay in the basement?

Come any time. There's a room with an attached bath upstairs that I can give you. There's no need to think further.

How can I thank you, Vinita. You've saved me from a lot of anxiety.

Just let me know in advance when you'd like to come over. Get the truck to transport your things late in the evening. Entry in this area is allowed only after six.

It's not possible to re-enter the institution of family once you've crossed its threshold. And why should you do it? If you allow no one else to interfere in your routine and comfort, why should you impose yourself on anyone? Why should you interfere in someone else's life? Why intrude?

Once again, loosen the soil of the same field, weed it, and sow it. What's wrong with that? Live by the strength of your own sweat.

The flat's gone, now that it's gone. Sold, just as it had been bought. The face of the old Wing Commander, the previous owner, peeped in through the balcony window and disappeared. He had his own reason for selling it, after his son turned up. His arrival may have been sudden, but the Wing Commander couldn't ignore it.

She looked uneasily at her bedroom. She had done nothing to make it more comfortable all the while it had been hers. The same old divan, table, cupboard with shoes peeping out from under it. It's time to collect them all. For how many years have you walked in them? Some were comfortable, others hurt the feet. Some were loose, the soles of others were worn. Some lacked polish. No, Aranya, this is not true. You must have one pair at least that is neither tight, nor loose—that allows you to walk with your head held high.

Kneeling on the floor, she collected her shoes and put them in a carton. As she took the box with the shoe polish and brush, old days swam before her eyes. Summer vacations. We siblings used to polish and shine our shoes every Sunday.

Such a long passage of time. Where did it go? It went in the buying of shoes.

She stroked her shoes, turned them around and asked: What direction will we take, you and I? Do you see an end to this journey?

Yes, where we all need to go one day.

There.

fifteen

Aranya took off her spectacles and covered her eyes with her palms. She craved for tea as the day's exhaustion spread to her hands and feet.

Get up, do something. You'll feel better if you do something. These are normal, everyday headaches. Don't let them get to you, keep them at bay. These are just ways to keep yourself alive, not the sorrows of romance.

How come you feel stuck in this, Aranya? It's asking to be ordered, not analyzed.

As she stirred the sugar in her tea, Aranya laughed to herself. These wrangles and entanglements are a thing apart from self-knowledge and epistemology.

What are they, then?

In truth, having a home provides the base for mental development and civic metaphysics. Living on the pavement or in night shelters, you can do nothing but carry baskets and pick pockets. The comfort of home is the basis of civic life.

The morning after an exhausting day of running around. Outside, the sun is shining. The curtains have been taken down from doors and windows. The bedding looks like it belongs to an inn. The agent mowed down her lush flower bed.

The place seems alien. The carpets have been rolled and propped up against the wall. There is a row of suitcases standing along the almirah. Cartons and wooden crates peep out of the study. On the wall opposite, hangs this year's calendar. When the next occupants have the place cleaned, it'll become part of a heap of rubbish.

How mysterious the patch of sunlight coming in through the window has always seemed. It couldn't be touched, but it had touched her body and warmed it over the years. It will fade forever for me, once I leave this house.

There's no dearth of warm patches of sunlight, Aranya. They'll come and say hello to you from some other window or door of some other house.

But when and where will that next house be found?

She went to the bathroom and filled a basin with warm water, placed it in the patch of sunlight filtering through the glass and dipped her feet in it. The faces of real estate agents who had been showing her around floated before her eyes. May be I can get into this profession, too? I'll need a hungry-eyed office, a telephone number, an astrologer, a pandit-tantric, a wrestler …

Aranya wiped her feet, and lifted the diary lying near her bed. There's still an un-ticked house and agent on her list. If for some reason she can't get Vinita's room, she'll need to look for a paying guest accomodation.

The telephone rang. It kept ringing, then fell silent.

It must be the agent, eager to heap on her the dues of the buyer.

The phone rang again.

Aranya continued to sip her tea comfortably.

I haven't come back yet; let it ring.

In the silence that followed, it suddenly struck her that it could be Ishan.

No, it could also be someone calling a wrong number.

If I always dial Ishan's number correctly, why should he have not called the right number?

This is not just a matter between you and Ishan. These are the subtleties of electronic exchange.

Aranya actually saw Ishan leaning over to phone.

She stood up. Quickly changed her clothes. Put on a pullover. Draped a shawl around her shoulders. Shut the doors and windows. Switched off everything in the room and stood waiting for the lift. She went down, crossed the block, and stood waiting for the next lift.

The comfort of living so close to one another. Freedom from taxis, autorickshaws, buses and the push and pull of things. Two blocks and the same kind of flat. Necessary for the story of any friendship, the ease of this geographical proximity. Or else there'll be the ticking of a taxi metre to quicken the heart beat. Why not take the stairs up?

I'll get out of breath. Don't forget, you've slowed down. You could get through this century; you could even get through the next, but you'll have slowed down. No matter. We'll be born again, there's no dearth of births. The likes of us are not likely to be freed from the cycle of rebirths. We'll have to come back in order to improve our chances the next time around.

The door of the lift opened and there stood Ishan.

Are you going somewhere?

No. I knew that you were coming, so I came to fetch you.

Aranya was surprised.

Perhaps this is a sign of something.

Ishan opened the door.

Aranya watched a shadow flit in the silence inside her.

She asked herself quietly: Someone perching on your bough?

Ishan stood, as if looking beyond the layers of her interior.

And even there, is there anything beyond the self?

Aranya understood some things, other things not.

The reality of someone, can we really comprehend it? How and what we focus on through the aperture of a camera must mean something.

Come, Aranya. Ishan moved towards the dining table.

I steamed vegetables with some cereal this afternoon, with a tiny teaspoonful of ghee. It turned out so well that I saved some for you.

If you feel like eating, I can bring it out.

I'll eat it with pleasure. How did you guess that I didn't have the energy to cook today?

Did you eat when you came back?

An omlette with tea.

It's not good to take such shortcuts, Aranya. And it's not good to eat too many eggs.

I don't eat them more than a couple of times a week. I do observe a reasonable number of dietary rules prescribed by the doctor.

More important than all else is eating on time. What did you do today; you weren't at home?

There were anxiety, doubt, concern on Ishan's face.

She said naughtily: I wanted to trouble you a bit. But my plans dissolved when I saw you standing outside the lift. Just imagine, how you would feel if you were to find me opening your door without ringing the bell?

How would that happen?

Well, figure it out! There's no way to come inside. And the windows are such that you can't but commit suicide if you step out of them.

There are some people, Aranaya, who kill themselves in bits and pieces.

Aranya got ready to shoot back a reply, but changed her mind.

There hasn't been enough time to get ready for battle. What he is saying is neither true nor untrue.

Isn't that true? Isn't it time to come back to the issue at hand?

Are true and untrue so far apart, Ishan? Why not borrow something from the values of our times? So that what is true no longer appears true, and what is untrue no longer untrue?

I'm asking about something else, Aranya.

She laughed.

Why so earnest, Ishan? Can't we imagine something romantic, thrilling? Particularly when the key to your guestroom is lying with a neighbour like me?

Could you be doing something just for the thrill of it, something you shouldn't be doing?

I may have been a dimwit years ago. But now there are pressures to take decisions which override everything.

Is it necessary to sell your flat?

Not 'is', 'was'. It's already been sold.

You didn't consider discussing it with me. As a friend, I had at least the right to know about it.

I had a lot on my mind.

I've heard about all that in the housing society meetings.

We could have found a solution all the same. You were set on having your way. Your virtues and temperament are your weapons, Aranya. But it's always wrong to rush into action without wise forethought.

There was no rushing, Ishan. Nothing unexpected happened. All that happened was that the flat was sold and I didn't get very much for it. The agent kept manipulating the negotiations for one reason or another.

The vanity of knowing better.

There's no need to quarrel about this, Ishan.

Silence reigned for a while.

The truth is that you're feeling scrutinized, thought Aranya. As if a familiar truth is being translated again. Sometimes the translation is so on the mark, it seems to be expressing your own thoughts, not someone else's. And sometimes, it seems so far away from your inner being, it makes your blood boil just to listen to it. There was intimacy and alienation at once in the words spoken. You've barely overcome your hurt before you've wounded someone else.

When I look around me, I feel it was right to have sold the flat. The papers were not in order; maintenance costs had become rather steep. And then there was its loan.

But there could still have been some discussion, consultation.

I felt that it was my headache alone. Perhaps I couldn't talk about it for that reason.

Ishan kept looking at the wall.

Aranya jumped up to leave: I'm off. I had come to get my mind off this for a while, but there seems to be no end to interrogation even here. Forgive me, Ishan, I feel besieged by housing agents.

Ishan leaned over and pressed her shoulders so she could sit down again.

Rest here today, Aranya. If you don't stay, I'll have to go with you.

And why, pray? It's not such a tragedy to have sold the house that I need someone at my side for sympathy and reassurance. Do I look so consumed by self-pity, Ishan?

No, Aranya. I am not being able to take this as lightly as you. I heard all that the agent did. I don't want you to be worrying about it all the time. Not tonight, at least.

Let's forget about the flat and talk about something else.

I am thinking of a parakeet from my childhood, Aranya. My mother had a pet parakeet. She had taught him to say: Rise and study, kid.

The moment the parakeet saw me in the courtyard, it would repeat: Rise and study, kid. I would give up playing and open my school bag. Mother would be so pleased. She would glance at me every now and then, and place a bowl of raisins, crackers, walnuts near me. I think of her whenever I see walnuts and raisins. She would be very happy when I did well in exams. She would make kheer full of nuts for me.

And your father?

My father was the ascetic kind. Once he left home, he'd be away for months and my mother would wait for him to come back.

Each time he left, she would ask: Do please let me know when you plan to be back.

This son of yours pulls me back. Whenever he crops up in my thoughts, I leave the sadhus and take the path home. Don't worry. I'll come back.

When I grew a little older, every now and then, on some impulse, he would quietly explain things to me.

One day, he said: The soul has two doors. One to go in from, and one to come out of. If you keep looking at the glitter outside, Ishu, the one inside will be forgotten. You won't even be able to recognize yourself. And if you keep crouching inside, then your 'outside' will become remote, so remote that it will be difficult to track it down.

Mother would react crossly.

What are you teaching your son, Pandit-ji. He's small, so impressionable still. Under your influence, he'll also wander off, like some lost sadhu.

Aranya looked at Ishan with interest.

Ishan asked: What was your father like, Aranya?

My father was soft of heart and deep. Miles away from intrigues of any kind. He had emancipated himself from being an Arya Samaji and found a master in Ramakrishna Paramhans. He insisted on just one thing: Look to see that right is truly right, and to right a wrong is in the interest of right. Go on about your father. Let's not pit the beliefs of the two fathers against each other.

After that, I got married. One day, I was indisposed about something. My father came into my room and said without any preamble: Don't ever think that your wife is outside of you, Ishu. She is a part of you, because you are a part of her; you are inside her not outside. She's educated, your wife. Now put your household in order and learn to sustain it.

My mother was peeling melon seeds on the balcony. Her hands stopped where they were. She seemed to be looking for something within herself. She was observing us intently.

I've often been arrested by that moment, Aranya. She searched for something inside herself and then looking inside us both. As if she couldn't fathom the meaning of this new stance coming from a man wearing the same old shell. She seemed to be asking herself—Has my simple straightforward husband managed to live in this way with his own wife?

A simple sadhu like my father who left home so often for the mountains—what would my mother have thought about him?

She must have been puzzled to hear him give the advice he gave me.

Ishan couldn't ascertain whether he saw sorrow or joy on Aranya's face.

I buy chocolates for you, but I never give them to you because of calories. Let's have some now. We get to revisit childhood when we hear the word 'chocolate'.

Aranya began to munch. She seemed happy.

Ishan glanced at his watch and said: There's no need to sleep in that empty flat. Stay over in the guestroom here.

Here.

Ishan slipped a cushion under her head and brought a blanket to cover her.

You won't worry so much while you lie here. Sleep comfortably.

I am feeling so much better.

Good night.

Good night.

chapter sixteen

Listened to Krishnamurti cassettes late into the night. My mind was running on two tracks at the same time. As if I was placing hurdles in the way of the majestic articulation and cadence of that philosophical voice. I was thinking about what you said. The logic and the mode peculiar to inter-relating. Last night's experience moved me.

It was unclear why I was so out of sorts at the meeting of the night with the dawn.

When I left for my morning walk, it seemed as if my ancestors came along with me. Maybe because I know that I'll leave no one behind me when I go. It will be a definitive full stop.

I've never seen you rue this, Aranya. Are you really so indifferent to this? But yes, knowing you has also released me from my solitude. I was lucky to be born here and now, and it was fortunate that we met, you and I, at this bend in our lives. We know that neither of us is happy or unhappy, Aranya. We're both outside our joys and sorrows. Because at this point, neither of us is waiting for any kind of joy. You had said in jest the other day that happiness is not a matter of the mind any more; it is one of financial capacity. If you have the money, it's possible to buy any kind of comfort. Diamonds, jewels, farmhouses … whatever money can get you … Are comforts the same as happiness?

You can talk acerbically about yourself, but I read and analyze myself with a kind of detachment. What isn't there, Aranya, cannot be. Given what there is, need there be any kind of lack? It's not me who says this; those who know the essence of being have seen the end of both being and non-being. You can't take the body for the soul just because it resides in the body. And, in the existence of these two, I am.

There's also the belief that this is my body. This is I, this is my brain, my hands.

That which pervades the body, is it not the soul? Is the soul an entity apart from the body? If the mind and breath are not the soul, intelligence and knowledge are not the soul, what is it? Why are these two experiences different from one another? Why does the person become extraneous to time and age and the potentialities of the soul come to an end? Why do mental and physical life come to an end? God cannot make another god. His laws are true and they are complete in and by themselves. That is why there is never any change in Him.

I am saying all this, Aranya, so that you know what is going on inside me.

You were saying the other day: Why don't we argue about metropolises, municipalities and such things and forget philosophy for a while? Why don't we talk of issues such as streets, water pollution, the sewer system, transport, electricity, water, and the aged citizens who will have turned into manure at the beginning of the next century? We'll need to acknowledge not only spiritual discoveries but also the very basis of scientific discoveries.

Yes, the successions of change never come to a standstill.

The mind remains caught up in experiences. Each experience leaves a mark on it. The impression of experience can never let the mind know the intense bliss of innocence.

As far as I have been able to gauge, you have little sympathy for those with a religious bent, though you understand the workings of human life .

It was you who had said: I haven't burdened my mind and understanding with too much clutter. Perhaps that's why I still retain the ardour to learn something new, and I expect the same of others.

I don't know what I expect of myself, and what of you. Could you tell me what you expect of yourself at present?

She picked up the pencil next to the phone and scribbled two lines.

Many thanks, Ishan. I won't stay for breakfast. I'll meet you this evening. I will have read these pages by then.

—Aranya

Back in her flat, Aranya opened the door and gazed at the room with vacant eyes. She felt neither hostility nor friendship at this moment of parting. She just stood there, with the reality of having sold the flat.

seventeen

Aranya felt as if Ishan had placed his hand on her head. A non-physical, noncomprehensible tremor.

The deep sleep of exhaustion overcame her.

When she opened her eyes, the room seemed to be suffused with dim light, as if she were in a dream.

She glanced at the clock. Three o'clock.

Sleeping on the sofa is not just a skill; it's a whole science. One can neither constantly turn, nor pull at the slipping blanket. It's like sleeping while not really sleeping

It's strange, this world of dreams. Fish-like memories swim to the surface. Barely have they come into consciousness that they disappear again.

For a while, the room and its walls had disappeared. There appeared a landscape stretching for miles. The room and Aranya were like shapes within that sequence of locations, as if emerging from a camera roll that had been waiting to be developed into scenes woven into one another. Like links in a chain of fulfilled and unfulfilled relationships, appearing in a solitariness descending from above. Like tongues of flame that crash and splutter even in this fire that has begun to turn to ash. A while ago, she had seen a deep, dense darkness envelope her. The golden glow of this warm bundle had begun to die down under a darkening sky. Shining on the glowing embers were not the yellow flames of fire but ashen layers of blurred grey. And who knows who was sitting in the circle assembled around it? The faces also seemed woven into one another. The arms and hands of the people sitting around the fire were missing. What on earth were they doing there? Who were they?

A form descended in her direction from the sky. With an unfamiliar gait, as if taking steps without using the feet, it came nearer and nearer—Who?

Aranya recognized him. My father!

The face and features were not distinguishable, but her eyes recognized him. How?

Before Aranya could rise to meet her father, she saw him walk away, beyond the darkness. From one end of creation to another.

Is this journey so short that in the blinking of an eye, my father can come from there to here, and then go back from here to there?

The blanket covering her had slid off. Before Aranya could pull it up again, her father disappeared into outer space, beyond the world of dreams. Where there must also be whole settlements of subtle-bodied dead. And house agents and brokers.

Aranya pulled up another cushion as, half propped up, she gazed out of the window. That's the way by which the wind comes in. That's the way by which my dreams must have blown in my ancient guests.

In a state of half sleep, she heard the dense, tremulous sound of the violin, tiptoeing across the gallery and echoing through the house. Malkauns. This midnight raga—an invitation to the pleasures of music.

Who was calling out to whom?

Whose voice was this?

There was something out there, turning narrative into counter narrative.

The notes in their sovereignty were marking their proprietary right, knocking at the ancient body and soul, stretching across years.

She looked at the clock. What? Four. No, three.

Aranya rose. Throwing a shawl over her shoulders, she crossed the gallery, and knocked lightly at the door to signal her entry. She sat down in the corner chair. The cassette continued to play.

The tremulous, heaving wave of sound played for a long time, intoning hidden spaces in the still room, caressing old souls in the intimacy of its reverberations. How hard to catch the melody, the beat and rhythm that span this interval in time, making both of them pulsate. The still solitariness of each seems to be undulating on the strings of the violin.

Striking terror at the unwanted, untimely, unknown—this melody of time.

The two ancients seemed like they were reliving old roles hidden in their bodies, minds, lives and souls. As if they were repeating the refrain of the base melody:

> There is happiness
> Because there is air
> There is sunshine
> There is water

There is the unblemished sky
There is breath pulsating in the body
It is still enclosed in living
When we get there outside it
And are finally done
In some portion or other
In some form
There will remain a memory.

We'll flow with the silences of this earth
When we are no more—
near memory
hovering over mountain tops—
In valleys, tanks, rivers, and waterfalls
We'll remain right here.

Endless are births and deaths. We live to die and die to live. So that we can begin again, be born again. Rise, and live again. Be reborn, again and again!

An ocean to be crossed, this universe.

Rebirth.

That which exists, wishes to be ever recognized.

That which is conscious, wishes to know all there is to be known.

It's a bliss to remain forever fresh. Be content. Be.

eighteen

The crowd stretches far beyond the gates. Mahatma Sadanand Maharaj stands tall on his jeep. Luxuriant saffron robe, the daily dose of opium the size of a grain of rice gleaming in piercing eyes, locks of hair dangling on his shoulders.

Mahatma-ji is explaining to his devotees: Dharma and faith are the deepest currents of this country. They're not only the source of life power, but also of political power. Only dharma can root out sorrow. What can municipal committees and city administrations do to make civic life happy? Not even God gives everything to everyone!

Victory to Maharaj Sadanand!

Preach to us, Maharaj! Show the way to those who despair.

The master speaks in deep, dark tones: We are all waiting, o devotees.

We shall wait.

Shall go on waiting.

Caught between Beginning and End, till such time as we are absolved. Till we take a new birth. Which will happen when our number is called out in the Almighty's office.

Mother Fate will herself give the signal to the parents-to-be.

Till then, we shall just linger.

But once detached from the body, the soul will set out to circle the globe. To inspect the global market, going from nation to nation, without a passport. To draw up an inventory of new trades for the future.

We'll need to make some provisions for the duration between birth and death. After achieving tranquility this time around, when we arrive again to carry out our tour of this earth, we'll find that our credit card, international visa card, house card have already been issued. And ration card? No, no, we won't need a ration card. That is only dealt out to poor Indians.

True, we may have to wait out the process of arrival and departure. There'll be a long queue of Indians waiting at the borders of this world. At one end of it, they'll be distributing condoms and at the other end, Indian children will be receiving polio vaccination—the drops.

One will need to wait to take birth. The same kind of waiting again …

But no worry. With the help of the relatives settled in the Beyond, we'll firm up our public relations with the ministries of the Lord seated above us. Only then will He send us to bask once again in the joys of this world. We'll need to take the required steps quickly. It is also possible that a bill against population growth may be passed in the Parliament Beyond.

Devotees, leave this matter to us. After all, saints and sages were foreseen for this very purpose. Cut down on the traffic between heaven and earth. As such your new horoscopes will be issued by the Public Relations office of the Almighty. We've already pitched out tents over there. Souls of humans like us are occupied in the same pursuit there. We'll bring them on board and have them facilitate this.

At the very least, we've taken care of this—that we take birth only via the womb of a high-class mother. Why would we abandon our old chain of birth, cultural mode and the codes dispensed by our law books? Countless are the times that our illiterate countrymen have beaten their heads against this. But the difference between cultured and uncultured castes has endured through the ages. Brahmins have been the agents of the gods, the lower classes of the demons. Which is why the gods remain pure, and impure the servile yavanas.

Our votes will be cast from this birth. They will be put in the same ballot box that our ancestors have kept safe, in order to protect their faith and beliefs. Whatever the powers-that-be choose to proclaim. It's only through us and our kind that our cultural heritage can be preserved in a long, unbroken chain, within our own internal network of relationships. How will these illiterates, who don't have even the alphabet, compete with us? How can these barbarians even approach the kind of threads that bind us together?

Are you listening? These are hard words. But even if they carry a bitter flavour, they are true. Only too true!

Forgive us, Maharaj, but truth no longer resides in this world. He's become the adoptive son of outer space. He's been legally adopted.

Truth has many forms; in this world they circulate in the form of lies.

Can't daughters be adopted by the heavens, Maharaj?

No, daughters must continue to stay on Earth. It is in the best interest of creation.

Maharaj, they've begun to consider themselves exploited and oppressed. They have begun to hear the voice of some lost soul in their bodies.

We know this denomination has been exposed to severe grief. That is the decree of fate. But now, some frightful force hired for the purpose, has cast a spell on it.

We take into consideration only the woman struck by heartbreak and pain. What of the others?

Mahatma, our law books have some passages, which bring out the nobler aspects of our mothers and daughters.

But bear in mind that a horse is tethered to a woman's body. Devotees, it is necessary to keep that beast under control. The truth is that it's only a woman's body. Its most profound sentiments are drawn from the bed alone. Thought is not its field. Which is why it is devoured by self-pity.

Maharaj, are men free of all of this?

It is through the soul of a man that the Greater Soul enters. Nature resides in the body of a woman. Maya is the second name of Nature. Please don't enter into a long dispute on this. If allowed that space, it will continue to grow and fester. Suppress it as soon as possible.

It's not always good to enter into dialogue and dispute. You are an ordinary householder. It's in your interest to hold onto belief and belief alone. Hold on to it.

All together now—victory to Sadanand Maharaj!

A devotee of Devi asked: Maharaj, may we also declare victory to the Goddess?

Why not? The Goddess is always paramount. We have no quarrel with the one who is paramount.

But, Maharaj, her electioneering thrives on other slogans.

No problem.

The tiny, multi-coloured bulbs swinging on two pillars began to gleam. Off and on they went. Red, blue, yellow lights.

Victory to Sadanand Maharaj!

Along with the slogans, a new frenzy caught on in the streets.

On the next turn in the road, Sadanand-ji's procession collided with another election group.

A leader from that side shrieked: Think, o virtuous ones. Think with open minds.

Electricity board, Water board, Housing board, Health board—they'll all become idle without work, if you entrust everything to the Almighty. You see this dirty canal. This is our national river, Yamuna-ji. The noble Mother Ganga, who brings peace to others, is herself bubbling over with dirt. Sadanand Maharaj, we'll need to do something. Will the divine powers soak up this pollution? Keep in mind that these citizens have rights.

Someone shrieked: Really!

The lungs of the citizenry are constricted with pollution. Throat infections plague our children. People's eyes are filled with smoke. There is lack of good water.

Listen, o listen …

Sadanand Maharaj screamed: The Upanishads say that the soul is free; it is constant, eternal and primordial.

Allow the state and its forces to do their work.

Stop this philosophizing. If we want mind, reason and attitude to raise Indian life force to the highest possible level, they'll need to understand the principles of justice, courage and compassion.

Your slogans reflect ways of thinking which are almost dead.

How can they intimidate you?

Pay close attention to this. The world is not illusory for us. It is constant. It is neither born nor does it ever die. It is always present, in gross or fine form. So why delude us about staying away from a better life? We have a Constitution to protect our rights. It speaks of the participation of people in democracy.

Parliament is the protector of our democratic values. We may well be backward, weak, of schedule caste, but the Parliament is ours too. We're also the inhabitants of this country.

The election season is over. Leaves fall soundlessly. Outside, the wind blows ever so softly. There is no electricity, only dense darkness, and the dusky glow of this body. Then it seems like the dawn is breaking. That we live to see a such a dawn … Isn't that reason enough to rise and stand?

nineteen

The truck that would carry her baggage was coming late. The entry to Khelgaon had been shut since the afternoon.

Ishan cast a glance at the baggage when he came in. There are too many pieces.

I've taken out a lot, but it's still too much for a single person.

They stay in sight, like old conventions. They're thrown out when our tales come to an end.

Ishan was quiet for a while, then he said: The knots and bundles of silent pain trail behind us. I have also been thinking of lightening my baggage.

Talking about the passage of time, one can say that rebirth happens more than once.

We enter a new body each time we move house, Aranya said irritably

They looked at each other with suspicion and fell silent.

I came to ask you out to lunch, Aranya.

Aranya responded enthusiastically: Always ready for such an invitation!

She grabbed her purse and they took the lift down.

Aranya went inside the restaurant while Ishan parked the

car. She found the corner table that she liked free, and breathed a sigh of relief.

I've been thinking since this morning that I'd like to lunch here and at this table.

Two can seem like a crowd if they are not used to each other.

Ishan looked at the menu: Cold beer?

Will you have one?

No, I'll go for fresh fruit juice.

Me, too. I've worked so hard what with all that packing. In grave need of vitamins.

There was a time when four days a week were spent in restaurants. I'm talking about the sixties and seventies. They're no longer around, but I'm happy that I'm still here and sitting with you.

Me, too, Aranya.

Let's order lunch.

Steamed fish. But you're vegetarian.

No, fish is regarded as a vegetable. I lived on it when I was abroad.

It was as if Aranya chose her words with care: This last lunch will remain memorable.

We're moving in opposite directions. Khelgaon is far from here; it may be difficult for me to find the energy to drive there.

Aranya laughed mockingly: It's easier for me because I don't have a car. Moreover, it's not so important for seniors to meet.

They laughed.

Tea or coffee?

I can have tea. But how about an ice-cream before that?

Aranya, won't it be inconvenient for you at Vinita's?

It shouldn't be. I will have a room with attached bath, and the rest of my stuff in the basement.

Ishan thought for a while. After a three bedroom flat, will just a room be enough for you?

I'm middle-class through and through, Ishan, and I take pride in that. I've been taught to move with the times.

Ishan was weighing each word: Don't laugh off what I'm going to say now, Aranya. If I say that a room with an attached bath and a balcony is also available for you in my flat...

Ishan, I need a day to think this over.

So many years have gone by. Where had we started and where have we reached. Who would have thought that in the autumn of our lives, we would meet, not like old acquaintances, but like new friends. We've lived in this city for so long. If we balance our accounts, will we know what we've lost and what we've gained?

Yes, Aranya, after getting to know you, it does seem that life is not a number on a bank account, which can be tallied simply by adding up digits. I am sure about this. Why not make our departure easy and natural? Neither of us will be inconvenienced in any way.

twenty

I assure you that not everything has been used up yet. The amount of water left in our pitchers is enough for the evening of our lives. Why shouldn't we stay by each other—with each other? The time, when we didn't know each other, is lost in the leaves of old calendars; that can't be brought back. But the few days that we have now can be made ours. You know Aranya, sometimes when in my mind's eye, I see myself walking down the college corridors, I feel I've become someone else. It feels more like remembering some old friend, someone closest to me. Now that I know you, I feel I've become someone else, Aranya. What would one call that? There must be a word for it.

As I dropped off to sleep, Aranya, you were probably awake. Now that you're sleeping, I'm awake. How different our daily routines, habits, ways of life.

You don't wallow in grievances and I stopped fighting fate a long time ago. I accept whatever fate decrees. Strange, the things that happen unexpectedly. The twist of fate that brought us together at this turn in our lives fills me with gratitude.

We've lived our times, spent them. Why not live the bit that remains wholeheartedly? I won't be able to say much about what I feel at this moment. I know you'll understand. You'll understand it the day you make up your mind to do so.

The experience that overcame me like a cloud heavy with water, I want to have it reach you without words. I've dug up this letter from an old file. When I found it, it felt as if even fate can make an ardent effort to reach out to you sometimes.

This letter written by a Yugoslav soldier from his deathbed says something that evokes respect. We may be able to derive some solace from the intensity of these lines.

My child,

As you gather strength to take birth, in darkness before it becomes light, I wish for your well-being. You have no form at this stage, no breath, no light in your eyes, but I'm filled with a deep certitude that when you and your mother come together in an unbreakable bond, you'll gather in yourself the strength to come into existence and draw breath. And once you emerge from your mother's womb, the special happiness and fulfillment of seeing and observing the radiant light of this earth.

It is the right of every human child to receive life. That is its goal. To receive body and soul from the mother's pure womb, appear in this world, and to keep struggling and moving towards immortality.

My child, may you be born through the grace of the maker of this cosmos. And may the light of your life remain aglow for a long time. May it benefit you, your childhood and youth. My blessings to you.

This is the period granted to all transitory beings from the one who is constant, to live here, to halt here.

It may be possible, once this tumultuous journey is over, to see the turns on that lonely road with the alert eyes of the watchman. So that you are able to give love and warmth to those who need them, to those who need sympathy and light.

My child, I wish that you have a childhood in which you may play to your heart's content, and move forward to take on a world that is not just filled with passion and attachment to the 'self', but one in which there is a search and struggle for those values, which mankind has striven to protect.

Along with trees and leaves, fields and granaries, rivers and streams, waterfalls, oceans, mountain peaks, keep alive the respect for heroes and great men. And along with these, keep protected the ability to confront any insult, the courage to fight and struggle against any injustice.

I know I have to collapse in a heap without ever seeing you, and that being born in my absence, you have to stand on the heap made of my omissions and sins. My son, forgive me. I know I'm leaving behind an untidy and tangled world. I take my leave of you. In my thoughts, my child, I kiss your forehead.

Good night!

Good morning!

A sparkling, radiant morning, gleaming in the crimson of the sun.

May it remain propitious for you throughout your life!

Your father, my son, whom you will never see.

twenty-one

Aranya woke up.

A tea tray lay on the bedside table. As she pulled it near her, a piece of folded paper flapped in the air.

She read it through. Then, read it a second time. Then, a third time.

She turned it around and saw a little line in a corner at the bottom.

Aranya, I'm going for a walk. There's lemonade. Tea as well. Breakfast will be ready by nine. There's no need to hurry to get dressed.

She looked at her watch. It was time for the arrival of the new owner of the flat.

Back in her flat, she looked into all the rooms. Everything had been cleared, but for a pair of shoes. My favourite pair of shoes, how could I forget you? No, I know why I forgot you. I have no need of you to get to the place I'll be going to next.

Will you give us away to the scrap dealer then?

No, memory will take care of you now.

And who will take care of *you*?

Aranya looked way from the shoes.

Then slipping them under the cupboard, she said: Perhaps memory …

twenty-two

The melody of time.

Time is a raga.

No, in time is bound up a medley of ragas.

Many songs.

In every song, its unique flow of notes. Resounding in the body. Soaking in and settling in the soul. Dissolved and absorbed into it, the intimacy and remoteness of each. A cumulus of light dawns within. The notes adorning rhythm and beat.

A raga is at once attachment and detachment. Warmth, love, and affection. Time finds ruses to entice, and leave you sad. The bird trapped inside flutters to be set free.

But not only sadness, tied with it, is a deep regard for all living beings.

True we were born and we have lived. Listening with rapt attention to the prelude of the raga, without being able to tell apart the subtle notes of a *tanpura*. In the same way, even if unable to understand the music of the other, we look for its resonance within ourselves. We can't tell whom we've listened to and whom we've pushed away, shoving them into anonymity, despite the deep and shallow experiences which enrapture the mind and body and make one sad or happy.

A deep attachment binds all seven notes into the scale of the raga and its *sthayi-antara*.

Udatta, anudatta, tvarit. High, deep and rapid. The many, many tone perceptions, note scales, and tonalities. And with each *aalap*, the flow of devotion and emotion, attachment-detachment, love-passion, hurt-pain, memory-erasure, gratification-immersion, pain-pleasure, sorrow-grief, joy-delight.

The raga of a life cumulated.

Aadim, *shadaj* and *nishad*.

The first note, *aadim*—the note of birth.

Shadaj—the note of youth.

Nishad—the last note of the human tale.

Childhood, youth, and the last note from the autumn of life—*nishad*.

Let them remain strung together as long as possible.

Only then do you get to the entire octave.

The melody of time.

This Earth

Angelika, a German married to Ishan's relative, worked with the Southeastern desk of Amnesty International. She stopped in Delhi on her way back from Kashmir to meet Ishan. Aranya also joined the dinner. Many inner voices echoed in the room.

Angelika's children, Vivek and Malavika, grew up in an Indian family. Ishan and Angelika, wife of his brother-in-law Suren Pathak, had a lot to say to each other. Sharing common family memories, they exchanged notes on the insights gained from them.

Angelika watched Aranya attentively. Raising her eyebrows, she asked Ishan: You still haven't been able to free yourself from destiny, have you?

Can anyone really be free of that, Angelika?

Aranya laughed: Perhaps I should leave. It'll be difficult to salvage the evening if we start debating about destiny.

Ishan said gravely: We can surely view life already spent like a story now.

Angelika teased: Ishan has to pay the price of having been born in Jammu-Kashmir. My husband's brother-in-law retired from the Postal Service. If his Maha-pandit, his Paramatma, had lent him support, he could have retired from the Indian Administrative Service.

Aranya turned to Angelika: Please go on, Angelika. That's news to me. Ishan never told me about this.

There's nothing much to it, Aranya. You get worked up so easily.

You're from Jammu-Kashmir, I'm from bordering Gujarat-

Pakistan. Why wouldn't I start at the prospect of those dizzying heights? But do elaborate on what Angelika was saying.

Nothing in particular. When I sat for the Administrative Service exams, I was ranked eighteen in the IAS and highest in the IPS, at number one. The Home Ministry checked with Jammu-Kashmir about this. Sheikh Abdullah was the Chief Minister then. He informed the Indian Government that Jammu-Kashmir was not part of the Indian Services. So I was offered the Postal Service and I accepted it.

That too with detachment. Ishan, you disappoint me. Did you do no running around?

No. But when Bakshi Ghulam Muhammad became the Chief Minister, an IAS cadre for Jammu-Kashmir was formed. The Home Ministry made provision for me in that cadre and sent my papers to the Government of Jammu-Kashmir for approval. Once again, what was not to happen did not happen. We won't go into the reasons.

The discussion turned to the issues of terrorism and human rights in Jammu-Kashmir, and the brutal narrative of the violence pervading the region. Amnesty International kept a watch on the violation of human rights across the world.

Is it truly so difficult to resolve the Kashmir problem?

Wherever it may be, in whichever country or region, military presence is bound to make the citizenry fight and rebel.

Drinking glasses were brought out.

I'd like to eat something before I drink anything, Aranya. I've not had lunch today.

Aranya took out brown bread and cheese.

Does this make the difference between native and foreign seem less?

Angelika's family has lived in India, she is used to Indian food. There is no difference between her home and ours.

No, no, how can you measure the difference between races by comparing food habits alone? Similarities and differences will continue to co-exist. And native and foreign responses specific to their locales, too, regardless of dissimilarities.

Angelika was alert.

The conversation turned to the United Nations Secretariat.

Aranya offered everyone a second drink, and made herself one.

It's being said that the Great World Powers are going to set up habitation in outer space. If only our nation were also in the queue.

Ishan turned to Angelika: Is this really going to happen?

Much will change in the next century. The technologically advanced generations of wealthy nations will go settle there. And poor, backward nations will remain behind on Earth. Aranya said impulsively: This means that the developed peoples, all white, will live above, and here on this Earth—the black, flat ones. According to reports, the brotherhood of developed nations will achieve two things there. The construction of a building for the United Nations Organization and the residential quarters of God. Whenever the UNO will feel the need, it will consult Him. The poorer races will have to look after this Earth, its earthquakes and tremors, Tsunamis and storms, and relentless terrorism. In short, all these problems will become the headache of the poor alone.

The diminishing population of this world will gradually lighten the load that oppresses the Earth.

Our population.

Our Earth.

Who will watch over its vegetation and greenery?

Who will protect it?
Mankind.
Mankind alone.
Nuclear weapons, never.
Never.

Krishna Sobti's Oeuvre:
A Palimpsest of Time

The Sweep of Krishna Sobti's work

P.S.

Insights
Interviews
& More...

Krishna Sobti's Oeuvre: A Palimpsest of Time

Samay Sargam is a love story, an autumnal romance between impulsive, anarchic, fiercely feminist Aranya, and gentle, sensitive, orderly Ishan. Poetic and prosaic, melancholy and sprightly, it is also a reflection on the passing of time, on the process of ageing and on mortality.

On yet another level, it is also the story of Delhi, the globalizing capital of a once new nation, and of its many layers, 'a *palimpsest*, a composite landscape made of different built forms superimposed one upon each other with the passing of time.'[1] No coincidence, then, that the year of the novel's publication marked the beginning of a new century, even as it bade farewell to the old.

Aranya writes, sitting in her bastion atop a high-rise on the eastern side of the city, about the transition of Old Delhi to New Delhi, and from New Delhi to what

[1] David Harvey, 'Urban Places in the "Global Village": Reflections on the Urban Condition in Late Twentieth Century Capitalism' in *World Cities and the Future of the Metropolis* (ed) Luigi Mazza (Milano: Electa, 1988), pp. 21–33.

it is now. The spiritual experience that marks Ishan takes place in Almora surrounded by the Himalayas, and includes people like Krishna Prem, once a Professor of English at Lucknow University, Shunyata, the Danish follower of Ramana Maharishi, and an American couple who had been friends of Frieda and D.H. Lawrence. The interweaving of Aranya's and Ishan's memories with the narrative of their gradually evolving relationship creates the palimpsest that is this slim novel. It is a palimpsest of time, a palimpsest of all the moods of the ragas Ishan listens to—calm, restless, angry, fearful, loving, happy, melancholy, fearful.

In the course of her life, Aranya moves from one Delhi to another, to finally settle in a trans-Yamuna residential complex, the past Delhis glimmering from the other side of the river:

> 'In the distance, the dome of Humayun's tomb basked in its arc of sunlight. The warmth of the winter sun lightly brushed her clothes. The endless drama of existence, and on such a vast stage.
>
> 'This earth, the sky, the sun, the winds, and us.
>
> 'What remained to be enacted on this stage?'

The partition of the subcontinent destroys and overlays the beauty and grace of Shahjahanabad:

> 'The trams and their tracks vanished from the streets in a wink. The row of trees lining Chandni Chowk were chopped. Stoves were lit on the pavements and dal and rotis began to be made there. The Lahore Gate of the Red Fort looked on in silence. As did the residents of Delhi. Parts of the wall encircling the city were swept away. The gardens on the outskirts of Old Delhi were rapidly sold off and, in no time, disappeared into the master plan. Villages underwent a complete metamorphosis. Three hundred and four villages of Delhi district were transformed into bigger settlements. Their identities were preserved in the names

of streets and small shops. And like them, we, young citizens of yesteryears, were transformed into the senior citizens of today.'

The destruction of this landscape alternates with the calm of a yet older Delhi, its ghosts laid to rest now, and recalled as Ishan and Aranya walk in Lodi Gardens:

> 'The trees beyond the mosque stay calm, laden with their own capricious branches. Who knows what the flocks of birds are saying to each other?'

Krishna Sobti possesses an uncanny ability to grasp complex changes in the geographical and social make-up of Delhi, its building, rebuilding, destruction and reconstruction, and to weave them, simply and deeply, into her fiction:

> '... when I sleep, I see long rows of laburnum, yellow blossoms and green fruit dangling from their boughs. I feel like a tree myself, covered in yellow and green. I used to walk on blazing, beautiful Hailey Road in the mornings and evenings. Perhaps that's lurking somewhere in my mind.'
>
> 'Friendships would the measure the roads; the destination was Connaught Place. Those bubbly, beautiful days, of picking restaurants. Standard, Gaylord, Volga, Embassy, La Bohéme, Nirula's, York, Ginza, Alps, Maidens.'

And now, in the discontinuity of the mega-city with no definable centre, the barren landscape of its exurbs dotted with jhuggis, the brand new roads which carry no memories of the past, the small DDA park is the one refuge of senior citizens who congregate there in the evenings, to silently document those who have begun to miss their daily walk, the terminally ill, and the wholly missing. The global connect goes hand in hand with the local disconnect of the inhabitants of the high rise apartment blocks with '... (t)hose who have no role to play in the new metropolis [and] are made virtually invisible by being "inserted into other discourses" or else they become demonized, as the enemy within, floating populations of urban nomads filling "pockets of hard, local realities," carriers of poverty, disease, drugs, crime, and violence'[2]:

> 'Ahead, there was a tangled cluster of jhuggis, huddled under slanted roofs made of sacking and blue and yellow plastic, just wide enough to hide your heads, and held to the ground by ends tucked into stones. From the ones made by shutting off the openings of barrels, emerges, along with the wet smoke from a coal sigri, the sound of a child crying. The dry sobbing of a child rolling on a half wet mud floor. The rain must be dripping in. The mother must be looking for a way to stop the leaking.
>
> 'Where will the child go after it grows out of the jhuggi? Will this Abhimanyu be able to escape his chakravyuha? Will he be able to emancipate himself from hustling narcotics or will he be crushed by the weight of generations? Will he be able to enter a clean brick house? Will he partake in the comforts of life? Will the imperial gaze of history manage to take note of him while there is still time? Will buying things at the Sunday flea market rescue him? Will he be able to fulfill his desire to buy new old-looking denims? Will the favours meted out by social welfare reach this puny citizen? Will the strength to sustain himself survive that long? He has sixteen to eighteen years to reach adulthood. It may be possible to become a politician in the next century. Who knows whether he'll behave like a hero or a villain?'

Aranya and Ishan share a deep awareness of nature, the tiny joys of everyday and their dry humour, but for all the consonances there are dissonances, in their philosophical preoccupations, in their respective styles of living – the quiet, controlled interior of

[2] Edward W. Soja, *Postmetropolis: Critical Studies of Cities and Regions* (Oxford: Blackwell Publishing, 2000), p. 151.

Ishan's apartment, the regular rhythm of his daily life, as against the anarchy of Ananya's existence and her acute awareness of social and political issues. They clash, sometimes bitterly, on the intensity and pervasiveness of his spiritual life, his belief in the security offered by the extended family, even as both are confronted by the insecurity and anxiety of what they observe in their circle of acquaintances, men and women, widowed or single, ageing alone, and vulnerable to the rage and violence of irate brothers and sons, waiting to take possession of what they have long regarded as their due: Damyanti, once fashionable, still radiating the sophistication of the once elegant Delhi and Lahore, driven to death by her son and daughter-in-law; quick, alert, cosmopolitan Kamini, who was famous for her beauty, who had studied in Benares and Allahabad, is slowly poisoned by her brothers' doctor in collusion with her young maid; Lala Prabhudayal, who had set up house with a woman in his old age in Meerut, whose sons have him strangled in cold blood. Can the family continue to offer protection in the face of the demands of modern consumerist culture, which entails living in flats designed to spatially accommodate only nuclear families:

> 'One's rights shrink with time … The warmth and oppression of living with the family, both come at once. The pre-conditions and predicaments of age. Then there is the shortage of space. The children aren't entirely in the wrong. In flats with just two or three bedrooms, two generations have to somehow make do with each other.'

Focalized largely through Ananya, with insertions of Ishan's thoughts, Shunyata's letters, and his own, this short, beautifully structured novel, tells both of coming to terms with age—

> 'Aranya stretched her arms and opened the window: Keep blowing, sun-drenched winds, as long as I am alive. Keep

reaching out to me. I wish my time here to be vibrant. All that bears fruit, all that is created—I wish to mark flowerbeds of words with that.

'No one is excluded from the pressure of existence.
Fire lives off the death of Earth
Wind, off the death of fire
Water, off the death of wind
And Earth is kept alive by the death of water.'

—and of Aranya's coming to terms with Ishan, with his sensibility and awareness. The tenderness but also the tensions of this relationship, as it reaches fruition, culminate in *Malkauns*, a midnight raga, signalling the meeting of two days on a calendar.

Daar Se Bichhudi, Krishna Sobti's first novel, was published in book form in1958,[1] and *Samay Sargam* was published in 2000. At one end of Sobti's range then, we have the story of a young girl in mid-nineteenth century rural Punjab on the verge of entering womanhood. At the other end, as we have seen, is the tale of an autumnal relationship set on the ever-expanding edges of Delhi in the late twentieth century. Krishna Sobti's writing captures moments of radical transformation in life and society always in a few strokes which are as bold as they are subtle. From youth or old age, rural to urban, feudal to post-modern, she covers all.

The early novels, *Daar Se Bichhudi* (1958) and *Mitro Marjani* (1966), with which she established her reputation for all time, display the same perfection of craft, the same clear-eyed lyricism, the empathy and detachment, and the depth of historical awareness, which

[1] Translated into English as *Memory's Daughter*, trans. Smita Bharti and Meenakshi Bharadwaj (Delhi: Katha, 2007).

have distinguished Krishna Sobti's writing from the start.[2] They simultaneously register and balance violence with tenderness, brutality with compassion. This balancing act is so delicate and subtle that to dwell on it is almost to distort it.

The 'dramatization of desire' of the women at the centre of Krishna Sobti's novels, their sexuality and their social transgressions, have drawn readerly and scholarly attention since the 1950s. For instance, the psychoanalyst and cultural psychologist, Sudhir Kakar, spoke on Mitro of *Mitro Marjani*:

> 'Her husband, the two brothers-in-law, and their wives, the husband's old parents, are all bit players in the dramatization of her desire, existing only to enhance and provide counterpoints to Mitro's moods and actions ... Mitro's husband suspects her of promiscuous tendencies, a belief that the spirited young woman does nothing to dispel. Indeed, she underlines this impression by the evident pride she takes in the fullness of her body, the sexual banter she carries on with her brother-in-law and the candid confession of her sexual hunger to her sister-in-law.'[3]

Yet, these moments of rebellion are seldom celebrated in Sobti's novels as mindless defiance alone. There is also an inbuilt narrative balance, never heavy-handed, never insistent; the touch

[2] For an analysis of the historical depth of vision peculiar to her, see also my essay on Sobti's *Dil-o-Danish* (1993), 'The Spaces of Love and the Passing of the Seasons: Delhi in the Early Twentieth Century', in Francesca Orsini's *Love in South Asia: A Cultural History* (Cambridge: Cambridge University Press, 2006). The novel is set in early 1920s Delhi, centred in Chandni Chowk, still buzzing with post-Mughal culture, but gradually anglicizing, the adjoining Civil Lines beckoning with their promise of a socially flexible life for women as much as men.

[3] In *Intimate Relations: Exploring Indian Sexuality*, Delhi: Viking, 1989, p. 14.

is light, however heavy the subject. Alongside the desire that threatens their stability, there is also empathy for the families which are being resisted, which fight for their honour as they see fit, and their at times gentle, at times violent efforts to prevent disaster. In *Daar Se Bichhudi*, Pasho recalls her grandmother's warning when she became aware of the attention Pasho attracted in the streets: 'one step out of line and your life will crumble to dust.'[4] And in *Mitro Marjani*, the elder sister-in-law tells the wild, defiant Mitro: 'Devrani, for daughters and daughters-in-law, the home and hearth are the farthest limits. If they cross these …'[5]

Mitro's mother-in-law remains considerate to the end: 'Beti, listen to me. Spend a month or two at your mother's, do all the necessary fasts and rituals. And I'll take care of things here. When my bahurani returns, all her wishes will come true.'

In the end, it is Mitro herself who recognizes that her mother's self-centred promiscuity has left her desperately alone in her old age, and she herself restores the balance she needs in her life.

Alongside this interplay of the personal and the social, of women young and old, it is worth recalling, once more, the historic depth that is so distinct a mark of Sobti's work. To turn again to her first novel, *Daar Se Bichhudi* was written when the wounds of Partition were still fresh. The memories of the violence which had accompanied the British conquest of Punjab in 1849, provided a palimpsest for that of 1947. The Hindu Khatris and the Muslim Khoja Sheikhs of mid-nineteenth century Punjab could get involved in bloody feuds, yet remain mindful of each other's cultural sensitivities and cater to them

[4] *Daar Se Bichhudi* (Delhi: Rajkamal), p. 123 . All translations from this novel are mine.

[5] *Tohellwith you Mitro* (trans.) Smita Bharti and Meenakshi Bharadwaj (Delhi: Katha), p. 20.

in delicate social situations. That culture seemed to have passed away forever.

In the preface to the new Hindi edition of the novel, Sobti speaks of the moment when the story first came to her, recalling the memories that squarely mapped the landscape of rural Punjab on to the cityscape of New Delhi:

> 'The days immediately after Partition. February weather with its flurry of leaves and wind had descended on Delhi. I always become restless in the month of my birth, shaken out of my roots before the month of Baishakh passes, not quite knowing what the dustladen winds sweeping through me are saying, sending god knows what sad, wilted messages, secreted from their dark inner recesses.
>
> 'That heartrending tumult again.
>
> Allah-o-Akbar.
>
> Har-har Mahadev.
>
> Partition.
>
> Division.
>
> 1947.
>
> '... Who knows what corpse-like shadows, from what towns, lost, wandering, scattered, had collected in the capital with what remained of the people from their localities.
>
> 'Crowds, sometimes in P-Block, at other times in the Ministry for Rehabilitation, sometimes in Purana Qila, Firoz Shah Kotla, Kingsway Camp. At other times at Turkman Gate, looking for livelihood, Kazi Hauz, Khari Baoli, Fatehpuri, Lal Qila, Jama Masjid. Chandni Chowk.
>
> '... I had passed the Sindhia House crossing and was walking on the pavement of Curzon Road.
>
> '... What was this?
>
> 'Shah Alami displayed itself before my eyes on the pavement of Curzon Road. Small and big shops, decked out and decorated, crowds of alert, adroit youth, the elderly and the old. Children

holding their mothers' hands. Hindu women, Muslim women, colourful chunnies, ribbons, bangles, vegetables, fruits, turbans, drying at the dyers. Suddenly, the glimpse of a face, like an inscription on the visage of the crowd.

'... What would be the name of this girl? Should I ask?'[6]

This is Pasho, a young Khatri girl of great sensuous beauty, who lives in Shah Alami, a village in mid-nineteenth century West Punjab. Her beautiful mother, widowed early, has defied convention and become the wife of a Khoja Sheikh in his high haveli. When Pasho, left with her maternal grandmother, regarded with suspicion and mistreated by her uncles, runs away to her mother, she discovers to her delight that she has a Muslim half-brother. But fearing blood shed, the Sheikh arranges for Pasho's marriage with a Hindu Diwan, old enough to be her father, but at once attracted to the young girl.

If the fierce antagonism between Khatris and the Sheikhs when it comes to marriage alliances is not glossed over, there is also a sense of respect for those to whom the difference is a matter of life and death. As her brother tells Pasho, when he visits her before she gets married, there had been a meeting between his parents and their mother's family, mediated by the elders of the village council. It hovered on the edge of extreme violence. But once the uncles heard that Pasho would go to a Hindu home, the meeting took a completely different turn. The elder uncle's eyes filled with tears; he bowed his head before the Sheikh: 'Sheikh-ji, you've given back to us the good name we unfortunates had lost once. May the creator be thanked, may He be thanked; our girl is now ensconced in a *kulin* family.'[7]

This short period of peace is followed by the death of Diwan-

[6] *Daar Se Bichhudi* (Delhi: Rajkamal, 2001), pp. viii–x.

[7] Ibid, p. 54.

ji, who fathers a son in his old age. The successive acts of violence that are visited upon Pasho culminate in the Sikh wars, the brutality of being sold into servitude, and the final defeat of the Sikhs by the British in 1849, after which Pasho lands in a *firangi* camp, to be tossed around by the joking soldiers. Only when her half-brother locates and carries her back home to her Muslim family, does she find acceptance, mirrored in her mother's words, that she is joined at last to the branch from which she had been so tragically separated.

Let us revert to the moment of creation of which Krishna Sobti speaks in her preface, recalling the violence of Partition:

> 'This is also battle. A war. Have we lost or won this war? Freedom. Freedom and Partition, both in one.'

And to the moment when a young girl spoke the introductory words of the story to her creator:

> 'One night, I was sitting at my table when someone whispered into my ear. May they live. May they stay alive.
>
> 'Forgetting accusations, complaint, pain, sorrow, bitterness, who was saying this to me, may all stay alive?'[8]

It was Pasho's voice, reflected in the opening of the novel.

> 'May they live. Stay alive. May they *all* live and stay alive.
>
> 'Good, bad, mine and not-mine—linked in whatever way to me—may they all live.
>
> 'Just a moment ago, I had wanted to say, let them all perish. May no one live, may no one stay alive. If I die, may I take everyone else along with me. If fate has chosen to forget this unlucky one, why should anyone else live?
>
> '... But if the creator filled my lap, filled it with prosperity, why shouldn't humankind also prosper? Why shouldn't mine

[8] Ibid p. xii and p. xiii respectively.

and not-mine live and stay alive? Those who held out their arms to help me in my adversity, and joined me with their branch, why shouldn't their households laugh and play in all their plenitude?

'May they all live! May they *all* stay alive!'[9]

How often has it been possible to say these words after Partition?

[9] Ibid, p. 16–17. Emphasis mine.

Acknowledgements

Translating Krishna Sobti's work is generally considered to be next to impossible; she works with so many speech registers – intimate, poetic-philosophic, political-public. I would not have ventured this attempt without her encouragement, warmth and engagement, and without the many conversations I had with her over the years. Shivanath-ji was almost always present at these meetings, and his generous support clarified many details. He gave me a copy of his beautifully illustrated memoir, which meticulously documents not only his own life and times, but also the history of the Indian Postal Service, from the late 1940s to the present. I would not have chanced upon them otherwise.

I will always remember Krishna-ji's gesture when asked about a word in a particularly moving passage of the novel; it turned out to be a misprint, one letter having dropped out in the Hindi transcription of 'van Gogh'. She told me what it was but also sent me some van Gogh reproductions, to bring home to me a sense of the reds and yellows referred to in that particular passage. It made me laugh, even as it brought a lump to my throat.

I am extremely grateful to all those who helped me in the

process of translation and I record their names, not only to thank them, but also to absolve them of any responsibility for what has finally emerged after so many months of toil:

Rashmi Sadana, for reading the first draft to smooth it out enough for further work;

Himani Dalmia, for going through the later draft to weed out the many awkward phrases that refused to go away;

Minakshi Thakur, for her intense engagement with the project, and for her invaluable help in polishing the final version;

and Ashok Maheshwari of Rajkamal Prakashan, for helping to resolve various logistic issues.

HARPER**PERENNIAL**

Harper Perennial presents special editions of its finest books in translation

Age of Frenzy
Mahabaleshwar Sail
Translated from the Konkani by Vidya Pai

A Life Incomplete
Nanak Singh
Translated from the Punjabi by Navdeep Suri

Mohanaswamy
Vasudhendra
Translated from the Kannada by Rashmi Terdal

The Music of Solitude
Krishna Sobti
Translated from the Hindi by Vasudha Dalmia

No Presents Please: Mumbai Stories
Jayant Kaikini
Translated from the Kannada by Tejaswini Niranjana

A Preface to Man
Subhash Chandran
Translated from the Malayalam by Fathima E.V.

The Secret Garland
Andal
Translated from the Tamil by Archana Venkatesan

Shala
Milind Bokil
Translated from the Marathi by Vikrant Pande

The Weary Generations
Abdullah Hussein
Translated from the Urdu by the author

Written in Tears
Arupa Patangia Kalita
Translated from the Assamese by Ranjita Biswas

HARPERPERENNIAL

Bhima: Lone Warrior
M.T. Vasudevan Nair
Translated from the Malayalam by Gita Krishnankutty

Chemmeen
Thakazhi Sivasankara Pillai
Translated from the Malayalam by Anita Nair

Ghachar Ghochar
Vivek Shanbhag
Translated from the Kannada by Srinath Perur

Hindutva or Hind Swaraj
U.R. Ananthamurthy
Translated from the Kannada by Keerti Ramachandra & Vivek Shanbhag

The Liberation of Sita
Volga
Translated from the Telugu by T. Vijay Kumar & C. Vijayasree

A Life Misspent
Suryakant Tripathi Nirala
Translated from the Hindi by Satti Khanna

The Sea Lies Ahead
Intizar Husain
Translated from the Urdu by Rakhshanda Jalil

Selected Poems
Joy Goswami
Translated from the Bengali by Sampurna Chattarji

Wild Animals Prohibited: Stories/Anti-stories
Subimal Misra
Translated from the Bengali by V. Ramaswamy

Wild Words: Four Tamil Poets
Malathi Maithri, Salma, Kutti Revathi and Sukirtharani
Translated from the Tamil by Lakshmi Holmström